This book belongs to

Children's
POOLBEG

❧ THE LITTLE ❧
DRUMMER BOY

❧ THE LITTLE ❧ DRUMMER BOY

Michael Mullen

POOLBEG

First published 1989 by
Poolbeg Press Ltd
Knocksedan House,
Swords, Co Dublin, Ireland

Reprinted May 1995

This book is published with the assistance of
The Arts Council/An Chomhairle Ealaíon, Ireland.

ISBN 1 85371 035 0

Cover design by Pomphrey Associates

Typeset by Print-Forme,
62 Santry Close, Dublin 9.
Printed by The Guernsey Press Co Ltd,
Vale, Guernsey, Channel Islands.

Also by Poolbeg

To Hell or Connaught

by

Michael Mullen

Don't be afeard, brother! These Irish traitors will be all driven beyond the Shannon. So the masters say. There they will rot in a great prison. Sea on one side and river on the other. It is a clever scheme.

So begins *To Hell or Connaught*, a story from one of the most poignant periods in Irish history, told by Michael Mullen as only he can.

Together with thirteen-year-old Bryan O'Dwyer and his courageous mother we travel through a barren landscape of untilled fields and rotting crops, hoping to avoid the English soldiery as fever sweeps through the villages and countryside. This account of the final extinction of the Irish aristocracy, the few who stayed to defy the Parliamentary army, is told with devastating simplicity. Slavery or serfdom – a stark choice!

Yet the book is full of courage, humour and hope, and with the Black Dwarf, Captain Kavanagh and his resourceful wife, Lady Margaret, and our boy hero, Michael Mullen has peopled a thrilling tale with unforgettable characters.

For Tim and Margaret

Contents

Contents

1

The King Arrives

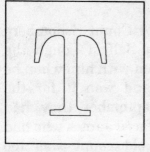he Norman Castle of Carrickfergus, intact in walls and towers, stood firm on the edge of Belfast Lough. Beneath the walls and jutting into the Lough, the pier swung out to form a safe harbour. From the first dawn when the sun broke the dark horizon with light, Tobias Parker, the sentry on the castle parapet, had looked towards the wide mouth of Belfast Lough. He had watched the bowl of grey fill up with summer light. He shaded his eyes with his hands and looked across the wide expanse of water. The only stirring on the sea was that of fishermen as they moved out in expectation of mackerel. At that early hour the air was fresh and light and smelt of brine. It was gentle on his body and on the scab that a wound had left on his cheek.

"It's more than mackerel we'll have in our

nets when William of Orange comes to lead us," he muttered to himself. "One battle will do it. Not waiting around with old Count Schomberg to take on James and his Jacobites."

He had marched under Count Schomberg since his first arrival in Belfast Lough the previous year. He had been with him when he stormed Carrickfergus and won it for the Williamite cause. In September they had camped at Dundalk and faced James who had fewer troops. But the old count was too cautious. He would not do battle. Then winter came and the fever struck. It was the first time that Tobias had seen the horrors of war and plague. Not as many would have died in a firm engagement as died that winter of dysentery and fever. The dead had been buried in wide graves outside the winter quarters in Lisburn.

Sam Gault had been drafted in to bury the dead. He was a small man, wiry and sharp-nosed. His skin was a sickly yellow as if he had been tanned in a leather vat. He could not count beyond twenty and had no reason ever to do so. He knew the size of a battalion and he believed that two battalions had died and two had been shipped across the wintry sea to

England to recover.

"They had the look and the mark of death on them before they ever set sail," Sam Gault told Tobias much later in the tavern close to the Castle of Carrickfergus as he drank his ale and reminisced on all that he had seen. Despite being a gravedigger he had a happy disposition, a personal view on everything, played a fife, and was a coward at heart.

"You believe in no cause, no cause at all," Tobias Parker had often told him. "You are Jacobite and Williamite if that is possible."

"I am that, I am that," he agreed, a grin on his face. Tobias Parker could not understand why he continued his friendship with this gravedigger. It was perhaps that he was the greatest fifer he had ever heard. When political arguments grew hard and hot in the taverns, Sam Gault drew out his fife and started to play. He could lead an army into battle or he could as easily lead a funeral cortège to the grave. When he lacked money he went to the city of Belfast and played at street corners with a false patch over his eye.

Tobias Parker wondered why he was thinking of an insignificant fifer when his mind should be on more important matters. It was evident to him that the next few weeks would be decisive in Ulster history. If James won the battle, which was most unlikely, then many Ulstermen would be dispossessed of their lands. If William won, then their claims would be firm and a Protestant king would have established his right to the English throne.

He had been a little confused by Schomberg's tactics during the last few months but he had been much more confused by the variety of language and uniforms. Troops had been drawn from all over Europe for this important war. Sam Gault, who knew a smattering of languages, could pick out individual words and identify the battalions and regiments for him.

And now the light of the sun was strong. The fishing smacks were more clearly to be seen and the stones of the castle were drawing in the heat. People were stirring in the town. They were moving through the streets and setting about their business.

Tobias Parker heard the tuck of a drum. He looked down into the castle yard. He watched young Jimmy Wright, dressed in his red military uniform, march up and down the castle yard, a side drum secured to his body by a strap across his shoulder. He was a boy of twelve. Ever since the age of ten he had wished to join the army as a young drummer. For two years Sam Gault had trained him in all the drum-beats. These drum-beats were varied and precise. Tobias Parker watched him move through the whole vocabulary of sounds from the general drum-beat to the retreat. He listened to the brittle sound taps filling the castle close. And then Sam Gault took out his fife and began to play Lillibulero. Jimmy Wright took it up on the drums. Both of them marched up and down the castle yard to the jaunty strains of the music.

Tobias Parker continued to look down into the yard at the two figures. The next time he lifted his eyes again to the horizon it was filled with distant sails. They had just moved onto the edge of the sea. And now beneath the sails he could see diminutive, faraway ships. He watched intently. They continued to mass on the horizon. He could not count the number. A great army was sailing towards Belfast Lough.

"Ships to the east. Ships to the east," he called down from the tower. "King William is coming."

People poured out of the houses and hovels within the shadow of the castle. They moved along the harbour and made their way to the bent arm of the pier. They strained their eyes and could see nothing at first but after some time they too caught the sight of approaching sails. They cheered and danced.

Sam Gault and Jimmy Wright, eager to be part of the excitement, rushed from the castle and were at the head of the crowd. Jimmy stood immaculate in his bright uniform of satin breeches and red coat. Sam Gault was wearing a Huguenot uniform which he had taken from a dead soldier. They watched the ships grow large and firm. The pennants fluttered in the wind and the great sails billowed outwards. Close to the harbour the ships drew in their canvas and under a light wind moved forward into the Lough of Carrickfergus. The crowd were now in awe at the immense fleet of ships which seemed to choke the harbour. The firm masts were like a forest in winter.

They could hear voices passing between the ships.

"Yon ship that carries the flag of King William's ship, watch it well," Sam Gault told Jimmy Wright.

Jimmy Wright looked in awe at the military might before him. All his young life he wished to drum soldiers into battle. Now a mighty army was ready to disembark. His heart was pounding with excitement. Sailors were lowering the shoreboats. He watched each movement with an attentive eye.

"It's the King who prepares to come ashore," someone cried. They watched the King's ship. Already several shoreboats had been lowered. They were obviously waiting for the King to descend into the royal boat, which was bigger and more ornamental than the others. It was manned by twelve oarsmen. A trumpeter stood at the prow ready to sound out his notes.

There was movement on the ship's deck. A ladder was suspended over the side and a man in a wide plumed hat descended. The trumpet cried out.

"It's the royal salute," Tobias Parker called to the people "King William is coming ashore. Hurrah for King William."

All along the arm of the quay the crowd took up the chant. The boats moved protectively about the royal barge. The captain of the ship barked an order and the oarsmen moved forward with an even rhythm to the shore.

"This is the beginning of a great and final war. Mark my words," Tobias Parker commented, joining Sam Gault and Jimmy

Wright.

But Sam Gault's eye was on more immediate things.

"Jimmy lad, have you noticed? The King needs a fifer and a drummer. In the excitement they have taken no heed to send one ashore. Down as fast as we can to the pier steps. It's not every day you get the chance to drum a King ashore."

"It's not forward of us Sam? Do you think I'm ready?"

"As ready as you'll ever be lad. Now hurry along." And with that he pushed Jimmy Wright forward.

"Make way for the King's drummer. Make way for the King's drummer," Sam Gault called as he pressed forward and made a path for the young boy.

And then they were at the granite steps that led down to the water.

"Play the general," he told him, "and as the King ascends the steps I'll begin the Lillibulero. We'll march him up to the castle with that tune."

Jimmy Wright settled his small drum at his hip and began the general as it was called by Sam Gault. The dry sound of drum sticks on the drum gave sudden emphasis to the important occasion. Suddenly everybody stopped calling out to the King's barge. A great silence, broken only by the drum sound, descended upon the quay. Jimmy Wright suddenly felt important. Behind him, part of the town garrison had formed into an ordered company. They stood in two serious lines.

The King was now approaching the pier. Jimmy could see the face of William. It was serious and bloodless. Worry lines ran from beneath his eyes. Their eyes met for a moment.

Suddenly the boat was at the foot of the steps. Several soldiers rushed up the steps and fell into formation, their swords drawn.

"And now the Lillibulero," Sam Gault whispered. Jimmy Wright did not hear him. Sam Gault was pulled from his position beside the drummer and pushed back into the crowd by the soldiers. But he refused to be set aside. As the King's head appeared just above the pier and there was a snap to attention, he pushed forward and began the Lillibulero. Jimmy Wright took it up on his drum.

The King seemed well pleased with them. They swung about and walked to the head of the soldiers, playing as they moved into position. Then they moved forward and drew the two lines of soldiers with them. The King and his retinue followed.

Sam Gault had a problem. So far everything had been perfect. He was leading the King and his retinue forward but where was he to lead them? And then it struck him. The castle gate was open. He would lead him into the castle and after that somebody else could take charge of the King.

They moved forward in great order. Jimmy Wright snapped briskly at the drums, his chest held out proudly. People were moving out of his way as he marched. He felt the power of the drum-beat in his body. Everyone present seemed affected by it. They moved up the cobbled pavement and entered the castle. The great crowd followed. And then they stopped before the entrance to the great tower. Some of the local dignitaries had hastily assembled and were waiting to greet the King. The drum-beat and the fife music ceased. There was silence and then a general hurray for the King.

Several speeches followed, including a short, hesitant one by William who found the English language difficult. And also his asthma was raking his chest like shot and he coughed and spluttered several times.

"He's no great talker," Tobias Parker said later when they returned to the harbour. By now its was filled with boats moving to and from the ships. They were surprised by the number of gentlemen who accompanied William.

"And tell me—who are all these fine gentlemen in flowery hats and suits of satin?" Sam Gault asked one of the sailors who was sitting on a bollard.

"The very flower of England and Europe go by and you don't recognise one of them. There be James Butler, the young second Duke of Ormond, and that talking with him is Charles Montague, the first Duke of Manchester," he said, pointing to two gentlemen waiting for their trunks to be delivered from a boat.

"And you see the fat one further up from you. Well that is Prince George of Daamstadt. He once nearly became King of Poland. And there are several others with William."

"Then we can expect a battle."

"Yes, a sure and certain battle. Count Schomberg has delayed too long. William will clear James and his Jacobites out of Ireland. William's flag will fly over Dublin afore August is out."

This was exciting news for Sam Gault. He

liked being at the centre of events and on the edge of battles. Now he was at the very centre of events.

By now those who were to disembark at Carrickfergus had come ashore. The great fleet would proceed to the younger town of Belfast at the end of the Lough and attend William's orders.

Jimmy Wright and Sam Gault were about to move further down the quay when a young soldier rushed towards them.

"Are you Sam Gault?" he asked breathlessly.

"Yes," Sam Gault replied, suspicion in his voice. "Who wants to know?"

"King William."

"And does King William know my name?"

"Yes. He inquired after you. He would have you and the young drummer lead him out of the town and to Whitehouse where he will meet Count Schomberg. Hasten. He will soon move out of the castle."

Jimmy Wright was excited at his new position. Sam Gault, however, hesitated.

"Surely this is the greatest of news, Sam. We have been chosen by William himself."

"I know lad. I know lad. But I have avoided wars for many a day. Now at the King's command I believe I am getting into deep water. I feel tingles in my toes and that is not a good sign."

"Hurry. There is no time for argument. The King attends you. These are my orders," the young soldier said.

They followed him up the quay. Outside the great castle gate a horse had been prepared for William. On either side of the gate soldiers stood at arms, awaiting their commander. Jimmy Wright and Sam Gault stood some distance from the King's horse and faced toward Belfast.

"And remember, when I give the nod start in to the general again and then into the march rhythm. We'll march two miles down the road and see if the King wishes us to continue. It's a good march to Whitehouse and I'm badly shod," Sam Gault complained.

"But we have been commanded by the King," Jimmy Wright told him

"I know. I know. The King cannot shorten a long journey, regal as he is."

He had little time to complain further. The King came through the castle gate and mounted the horse. Jimmy Wright began the general and almost immediately went into march beat. The King moved forward, flanked by his soldiers, while behind him other dignitaries joined in the cavalcade. Little did Jimmy Wright know then that he was setting off for a war.

They were foot-weary when they reached Whitehouse. They had drummed and fifed the whole distance. Crowds lined the roadside, drawn by the news that William was marching towards Belfast.

When they were finally discharged by William they sought refuge in a barn. They lay down on the hay exhausted, their feet burning in their shoes.

"I have no taste for all this marching, Jimmy. I'd prefer playing in some common alehouse. I'm not made for the grand occasion," Sam Gault said, taking off his boots and stroking his hot and scored feet. He held his boot up the light and then pushed his finger through a hole in the sole.

"Do you think that King Billy will pay for my boot? I have played him many a mile and nothing to show for it."

"Careful of your language. A King deserves every deference," Jimmy Wright told him. "I was always told to respect my monarch at the almshouse run by Mrs McGuzzle. We prayed each night for the good King of England."

"I am a gravedigger. When I am not a grave-digger I play the fife. I know nothing of Kings. As I said, I was not born for grand occasions."

"Then you are a bad man, Sam Gault, and should be full of shame," Jimmy Wright told him. "Many would be greatly honoured if they played for the King."

"I'm a poor man, Jimmy, but I'm not a bad man. I've lost a shoe already and nothing to show for it. I'd say that Billy the King has forgotten about me. I'll kip down now and sleep."

He rolled up into a ball and fell asleep on the hay. Soon he was snoring heavily.

While Sam Gault was snoring heavily singular decisions were being made at Whitehouse. The generals had gathered to pay their respects to William. He received them cordially. The only exception was Count Schomberg. The old Count, now in his seventy-fifth year, moved with some difficulty. All his adult life he had been a soldier. Now, carrying the scars of many battles, he presented himself to the King. His reception was cold. The King treated him with indifference. He now took personal control of the army in Ireland. He talked briskly with the generals. He wished to know how many

men they could put in the field and how many
field guns they had at their disposal. Also he
wished to know how an army would be
victualled during the summer. He had no wish
to engage in a long campaign. It cost money
and he had business to attend to in England.
This battle would secure his new throne and
would settle any challenge James II might
make to his position as sovereign of England.
Great maps were laid out on the hunting
table. William pointed at various positions on
the road between Belfast and Dublin. He
could quickly understand a map.

"What river is this?" he asked, pointing to a
river with a double curve.

"That, my Lord, is the Boyne," Gustavus
Hamilton, commander of the Enniskillen
regiment, told him.

"Is it fordable?"

"Yes. At Oldbridge, Your Majesty."

"I note that there are hills above both
banks. Very suitable for artillery," William
remarked. "When we defeat James and cross
this Boyne river, then the way will be open to
Dublin. This must be our object. A quick
movement towards the south. There will be no
delays. My army will not winter in Ireland. I
shall now move towards Belfast."

While Sam Gault slept many military decisions had been taken. Jimmy Wright in the meantime had left the barn and walked amongst the soldiers gathered in the cobbled yard of Whitehouse. They were only part of the great army. They had come with their generals who were gathered in the impressive mansion. He looked in awe at their bright uniforms, the silver buttons, the jangling sabres and high leather boots. They spoke only of war and the money William had brought in great chests to pay them their wages. They would have many a glass of wine and keg of ale on what was owed to them. They felt confident that William would bring the campaign to a successful finish.

The meeting in the great house finished. The generals with their plumed hats and fine long coats emerged through the wide doorway. They made directly for their men, mounted their horses and prepared to accompany the King to Belfast. Immediately Jimmy Wright rushed into the haybarn and shook Sam Gault awake.

"I was having such a grand dream," he complained. "I owned a mansion on a hill and I was attended by servants in silver satin. I even had my own white horse."

"William is about to march on Belfast. Hurry."

"I'll not walk another mile. My feet have suffered greatly already in this cause. I'll be carried. I'll not walk."

A great carriage was drawn into the yard. King William entered and ordered it forward. It was followed by several other carriages bearing the dignitaries who had arrived with William. And behind them others joined in. Finally the baggage animals moved sluggishly out of the yard. Sam Gault drew himself up into a haycart and pulled Jimmy Wright up after him.

"This is fodder for the horses and we are fodder for the cannon," Sam Gault remarked. "I'm going to sleep. Perhaps I can take up where I left off in that dream. Wake me when we enter Belfast."

And so, in the back of a slow haycart, the road to Carrickfergus getting longer behind them, Sam Gault, fifer and Jimmy Wright, drummer boy, went to the beginning of a war.

2

The Final Feast

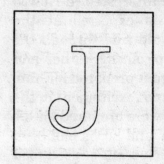ohn Desmond looked down from the narrow parapet of the castle tower. He often passed up the stone steps when he escaped from his old teacher and opened the trapdoor which let on to the flat leaden roof. From this high point, he could peer through the embrasures and survey the sweeping countryside about him. To the south lay the shallow line of the blue Dublin mountains. Beyond them lay Wicklow, with its mysterious glens where men could shelter from the law. To the north, on a very fine day, he would see the blue sweep of the Mourne Mountains. To the east lay the firm presence of the the hill of Howth. He had frequently visited Howth Castle and sat at table in the great dining hall with the Lord of the high and rugged hill and his family. Frequently he had

rode home along the wide sweeping shore with its sand dunes, urging his pony across the hard, ribbed sand.

But to-day he was not interested in Howth Castle. King James was expected at the Desmond Castle. He would ride through the gates with his retinue to join his father and mother at the great banquet prepared for him. All day there had been great excitement in the kitchen as meat and fish were prepared for his arrival. Fresh vegetables and herbs had been cut in the garden. The rich scent of good food filled the kitchen. The best wine, in dusty bottles, had been brought from the vaulted cellars and carefully set out on the great black oaken sideboard. His old teacher had been called upon to prepare a welcome in Latin and had spent the day in the library racking his brains in search of silver phrases with which to praise King James, up to recently King of England.

"I think your allegiance is misplaced, Matthew," his mother told his father when they sat before the great fire. "I may be a woman and not versed in the ways of the world. But I know James is not interested in Ireland. He may be a Catholic but he was a rash King while he ruled England. You are foolish to follow him or listen to his words. You have too much to lose, too much."

"Wife, you understand little of the ways of war," Mattew replied. 'The final battle must be fought here in Ireland. It will give us firm and final title to our lands. The confiscated lands of our friends will be restored. William of Orange is a usurper. He has no call or claim to the throne. James is rightful King and to him alone I will give my allegiance."

"These foolish words will lead both you and my sons into a final battle. I brought them up to lead fruitful and pleasant lives. Will you place their lives and these estates and woods in jeopardy? At this present moment not even the Pope sides with James. He is a pawn of the King of France," she protested.

"Enough of this talk, wife," Matthew told her.

"I'll not hold my peace Matthew Desmond. I'll have an equal voice here. James is a stupid man. Will you have my sons follow this man into the fatal battle?"

"The Desmonds are soldiers, wife. They will follow James's drum."

"And a sad drum will follow them from the field."

Her voice was firm. Matthew knew how she

distrusted James and his promises. She had
kept abreast of all that had happened since his
arrival in Ireland. She had questioned her
husband on each meeting of the new council.

"He has no interest in your cause. Mark
every word I say. Not even the Pope favours
him because the Pope does not favour Louis of
France. Your allegiance is badly placed I, tell
you. Join William. Your cause would be better
served."

"I will not hear such blasphemy in my own
house," his father finally cried out, not
wishing to listen to her arguments. He
stamped out of the house in anger and walked
up and down the walled garden, his hands
clasped behind his back, the veins of his
forehead knotted in thought.

But John Desmond's three brothers were
not caught up in such worries or thoughts.
Immediately news arrived at the castle that
James had landed at Kinsale, they donned
their their fine clothes, buckled on their
weapons and set out to meet him on his way to
Dublin. They had been with him when he
marched into Dublin on Palm Sunday. All
along the route men had flocked to the
standard of James. All southern Ireland was
sympathetic to his cause. However, the

colonists of Derry and Enniskillen held out
against James. They were dour and tough and
would endure any hardship for their beliefs
and lands. That was a year ago. Since that
time the Desmond brothers had remained
close to James. They were flattered by his
presence and believed in the dream that he
would restore all lands confiscated by
Cromwell. They were young and spirited men.
They took excitement in the movement of
troops, the preparations for battle, the
planning and the intrigue of war. They could
endure the rigours of the field and sleep under
wet canvas on damp undersheets. Yet they
were always turned out in the most elegant
fashion when they rode beside King James's
coach

Now James II, the deposed King of England,
would visit the castle for a great supper before
he moved north to take command of his army
at Ardee.

John Desmond continued to look towards
the city of Dublin. He had been on the
battlements for two hours looking down at the
miniature world below him. The sun was
setting behind the trees after the long June
day when he noticed the movement of troops
on the southern road. He watched intently as

a cloud of dust curled up behind the outriders who escorted the royal coach. James II was coming to the feast.

He rushed down the tower stairs calling out, "The King is on his way. He is on the south road."

He rushed through the rooms with the news. Excitement began to stir in everybody's mind. Many had their doubts concerning James II but now these were swept way. They were over-awed by the thought of his arrival. Some of the servants made their way to the upstairs rooms and peeped from behind curtains. Others poured outside and ranged in a crescent shape before the great doors. They were dressed in their cleanest and brightest livery. No King had ever visited the castle before and the grandeur of the occasion held them spellbound.

They looked down the long avenue. They could hear the thunder of horses approaching as they beat out a tattoo on the surface of the wide avenue. And then, some hundred yards from the house, the coachman reined the horses and they fell into a tinkling canter. The outriders drew back to let the coach move forward to the gravelled court. Quickly Matthew Desmond moved forward, opened the gilt carriage door and helped James II to descend.

James II wore a wide-brimmed hat with a long elegant feather. A rich wig fell over his shoulder. A white ruff about his neck emphasised his sharp and aristocratic face. His sensual mouth seemed arrogant as if the presence of so many people was distasteful. His sharp eyes looked at the façade of the castle. For a man of fifty-seven years he had a sharp step and young John Desmond knew that he was courageous and firm on the battlefield.

"You are most welcome to the house of Desmond, Your Majesty," his father said by way of welcome.

"Your sons have served me well, Sir, during the last year. They are indeed worthy of their fine name. Let us hope that they will win fame in the coming encounter," James replied in a distant and formal voice.

"Thank you, my noble King."

Followed by James's retinue, they passed through the arched door of the house and entered the great hall. Lady Catherine Desmond was waiting to greet the King. Despite her personal feelings towards the monarch, she curtsied. Then the whole company entered the great oak hall, where for two centuries the Desmonds had feasted in a spacious room panelled in Irish oak and with great beams and rafters bearing the pitch of the roof. On the walls hung the coats of arms of the various families that had married into the great house. The Desmonds were well established in both the Irish and the Old English traditions.

James did not immediately take his seat. He stood for some minutes and admired the coats of arms. He asked Matthew Desmond to explain their significance. Perhaps James II did not understand the great and mixed bloodlines that had shaped the fortunes of the Desmonds. He was, however, aware that he could not grant the old Irish or the old English their wishes if he won the final battle. They sought too much. This he could not reveal to them.

However, he must not lose their alliance. They had a confident belief in him. He carried their hopes.

When all had taken their places the great feast started. Servants carrying large trays of warm food entered the hall and placed them on the the tables. James was privately served. He ate only small morsels of food, which he washed down with red wine. He turned to Matthew Desmond and commended him on his cellar.

"The wine, Your Majesty, has been set down many years ago and has been attending you for all that time."

It was a delicate compliment that touched James's refined mind. He had not expected to find such delicate tastes in Ireland. He sat at the head of the table for an hour and then begged to be excused. With Matthew Desmond and many others he made his way into the great study. It was a room lined with expensive books. On the great table military maps had been set out. James stood before them and the others gathered about him. John Desmond, who had slipped into the room, listened to the serious conversation of these men who had left the great feast.

"What news have we of William?" James asked a young soldier who had appeared during the feast. His clothes still carried the dust of the road.

"He has just arrived at Belfast and attends guns and ammunition from England. He is not pleased with Duke Schomberg's delays. He is eager to press on for a final battle," the young soldier explained.

"How many pieces has he?"

"Forty, perhaps fifty."

"Then our position at Ardee is weak. We must draw back to the River Boyne. We have the protection of the water and Drogheda is well defended," the King said decisively.

"Should we not hold Moyra Pass to the north of Dundalk? Troops marching from the north could be held indefinitely at this position. William could be prevented from coming south. A long delay at this point would be to our advantage. It would weaken William's position in England and a victory by King Louis on the continent would leave the south coast of England exposed," an aide advised.

They studied the map closely for some time with intense expressions, trying to imagine it filled with moving masses of soldiers. They looked at the mountains and the marshy places where cavalry might get bogged down and be exposed to withering shot.

"You know this country, Matthew Desmond," James said. "Could we hold William at this pass?"

"We could, Your Majesty, if William would conveniently march through it. But he knows the danger that lies in this narrow defile. He can sweep through the country in an easy half circle and approach Dundalk through Armagh and Castleblaney," he explained, pointing to the longer route.

"Then the Boyne must be our best defence," James said

"I believe that we should move westwards along the Boyne," Patrick Sarsfield advised. He had followed James to France and landed with him at Kinsale. "Prolong the engagement. Keep William in a state of alert but never face him in battle line. That is what he seeks. That is what we must avoid. Another winter would favour us."

"That would leave Dublin exposed. If William captures Dublin then he will claim victory. We will be walled up in Connaught behind the Shannon. No, we must meet him in the field," James replied. "Tomorrow we will move to Ardee. In the meantime let us return to the great hall and join in the merriment."

As soon as they filed out of the library John Desmond went to where the King had stood. He drew a chair forward and stood upon it. He looked at the great map spread out before him. Imitating the King, he looked seriously at the ink markings on the large crisp sheet of paper. He began to do like the King, prodding at the map.

"We shall move our troops beyond the Boyne. Young Captain John Desmond shall lead the first cavalry charge against William. He is my very best man," he said in a deep mannish voice. He imagined the thunder of hooves, the mass of moving horses, whinnying and snorting as they charged forward, the puff of smoke and the massive cannon-balls ploughing into the hills, the clash of swords as the two armies locked in combat. He jumped from the table and, drawing his small ornamental sword, began to parry and to thrust.

"Long live James, rightful King of England. Death to the usurper William!" he cried.

And then his brother Philip entered the room. He came to retrieve his hat which he had forgotten.

"And how did you succeed in entering the room. Surely you know that King James has just been here," Philip said sternly.

"I know. I was here, hidden behind the curtain while he spoke to you. I listened to every word. Now I know definitely that there is going to be a battle and it will be very soon. I wish I could go with you," he told his brother.

"And what would you do?" his brother

asked.

"I would ride my pony with you. I would charge with drawn sword and I would cut down William's cavalry."

"All by yourself?"

"With the help of my brothers," he replied smartly.

His brother swept his sword from its scabbard and began to parry with his brother John. The young boy came forward, pushing his brother towards the wall. And then with a quick gesture his brother whipped the small sword from his hand.

"It is time for bed," he told him. "Young soldiers need sleep."

"But can I not see James once more before I go to bed?"

"You may observe him from the balcony. I shall go with you."

The small balcony stood above the great hall. The tables had been set aside and an orchestra sat on the dais. James and his officers were engaged in a gracious dance with the ladies. It was one of the new dances introduced from England. John Desmond did not particularly like it. It seemed effeminate. He believed that soldiers should always be firm and serious, ready for battle and practising their horses instead of dancing to some slow tune. He lost interest in the proceedings. His brother took him by the hand and led him to his room. When he was undressed and in bed Philip sat beside him and told him of his adventures during the last year.

He fell asleep to the sound of music. In his dreams he was riding beside King James on a white charger.

Late that night James's carriage drew up again before the castle. The guests poured out through the great door and gathered in front of the house as James took his leave from Matthew Desmond and his wife. He was in a pleasant mood. The rigid and aristocratic lines of his face had softened during the night.

"Soon darkness between day and day will be very short," he said to Matthew Desmond as he looked towards the eastern sky where there was a grey suggestion of light.

"Yes, Your Majesty. It will make for a long battle," Matthew replied

"Yes. It will give little cover to those who retreat," James laughed.

"Let us hope it will be William when the time comes," Matthew Desmond answered in a bantering tone.

With that King James mounted into the carriage and the door was closed. He waved lightly to his host and the guests as he passed forward towards the avenue.

The guests returned to the great hall. Matthew Desmond took his harp and began to play for them. His fingers moved nimbly across the strings. He played old and sad Irish airs which had been been heard in the great halls during the centuries. They carried with them a longing and a sadness which King James would not have understood. Somewhere in the music was the reason why the Desmonds were going to war. About Matthew Desmond stood his sons, eager and strong young men, who listened intently to the music played by their father.

It was very late when the gathering broke up. The guests spoke in muted tones before they took their leave. They knew that there was going to be a decisive battle and many had forebodings as to its outcome.

They toasted each other before the final departure.

"To the old cause and may we meet beneath this roof, hale and well, a year from now," Matthew called

The Desmonds had only a little time to

sleep. At eight o' clock they were dressed in light armour, had their swords belted about them and were ready to eat a light breakfast. John Desmond had been awake before his brothers. He too had put on his small cuirass and sword and was waiting for them in the great hall.

Later when they were ready to depart, the groom led their horses around to the main entrance. Catherine Desmond stood at the main entrance. She was dressed in a long robe and her expression was both serious and sad. One by one she embraced her sons as they left the house and mounted their horses. Finally, she could contain her tears no longer. She threw her arms about her husband and wept.

"Never fear. We shall be back," he told her. "I have been to many bloody engagements and I have always returned. So do not fear."

She continued to weep. Then she dried her eyes and said goodbye to her husband.

By now John Desmond had arrived from the stable yard on his white pony. He was to travel with the party as far as Dublin and then return home. He took his position beside his brothers and father with pride. Together they swung away from the house, moved into formation and set off two by two down the avenue at a trot. They built their pace up into a gallop and soon they were passing along the road to Dublin. John Desmond felt elated as he rode with his brothers and father. He wished that he was going to the battle. But soon the walls of Dublin came in sight.

"But can I not visit the barracks and watch the army march out of the city?" he pleaded with his father.

"No, I forbid it. The times are dangerous. A young rider in Dublin could be whipped off his pony and never seen again. No, you have come to the gates of Dublin. It is time to return," his father said sternly. "This is no place for a young boy."

John Desmond felt hurt at the remark. With his sword and his cuirass and pony, he felt equal to his brothers. He longed to go to battle with them. However, he said goodbye and turned his horse homewards. He had not rode far down the road when he decided to return to the city. He slipped in through the northern gate. He had to be cautious. He was familiar with the main streets of the city, but there were narrow lanes where he could fall foul of thieves.

As he moved through the main streets, he noted that the city seemed choked with soldiers of different countries. They wore various uniforms and used a variety of languages. Some of the footsoldiers were drunk and abused him calling him a "young popinjay."

They shook their menacing weapons at him.

"Drink well," they called to each other. "Tomorrow we may sup with the devil. Drink well, for battle is thirsty work and the day will bake our tongues to leather."

John Desmond felt that they were beasts of the field and without souls. They had no great feelings for battle or honourable desire to serve James II or the old cause.

And then a rider passed through the streets sounding a trumpet. Immediately, the captain of each regiment began to beat his men into some sort of order. They lined up in shapeless masses on the road, some carrying scythes on their backs, others with cudgels.

A captain in armour rode past with his sword drawn.

"Into formation you scum or I will run you through," he called abusively at them. One recruit was still at a tavern door drawing ale from a small barrel. The captain brought the flat of the sword down on the soldier's back. The blow was so severe that he stumbled onto the barrel. He spat two teeth onto the ground.

"Me teeth. I lost two of me teeth," he wailed.

"Into the ranks. Before the week is out you may have lost two arms," the captain called.

Finally, the ragged and poorly armed men formed rough ranks. They looked more like penned cattle than soldiers. A drummer tucked in the distance. They straggled forward on their way to war.

John Desmond looked at the raw recruits who had been pressed into battle. Many of them had been released from jail on condition that they joined the army. It was a choice they quickly made. Along the road to Ardee they would slip into the woods and escape. They had no heart for a battle. They cared little whether William or James ruled Ireland, or whether it was a Catholic or Protestant who sat on the throne of England. They would not worship at chapel or temple.

John Desmond took a short-cut towards the northern gate. Here from the shadow of a cart he watched the flower of James II's army move forward on their chargers. They looked confident and the plumes on their hats and their fine velvet clothes made the occasion a light and gay affair.

Behind the cavalry came the French Foot. It

was said that they numbered six thousand men and were well favoured by James II. They were soldiers who had been tested in many battles and they had grim and serious expressions on their faces. They were well armed and marched firmly.

Behind them came the raw recruits followed by artillery guns drawn by large horses and then the general baggage. John Desmond watched a great army on the move. Sadly he turned his horse for home. As he rode through the open countryside he reflected on all that had occurred during the last few days. He had been in the presence of a king. He had been at a secret battle-meeting in the library; he had ridden with his brothers and father to join the army. He had watched the army pass out of Dublin on the way to the north. He knew that the time for waiting was over. Soon the final battle of the kings would be fought. He would be on the battlefield when James defeated William.

3

Battle Talk

am Gault, fifer and gravedigger, and Jimmy Wright, drummer boy, now lacked importance. They were part of the great Williamite army gathering in Belfast to move south. They had been conscripted into the army and had received their first meagre pay.

"I should never have fifed William up the quay in Carrickfergus. It were a bad and serious mistake," Sam complained after he had taken William's pay.

"But you will be remembered when they come to set down the events of the battle," Jimmy comforted him.

"It will not matter when I'm dead. My habit was always to be part of the crowd and when I did go to battle it was at the tail end of the last regiment and with my spade. Now in a fancy red coat with buttons I fife the cavalry up and down the square every hot summer's day. It wears me out, Jimmy, wears me out, and it's too regular. It suits me not at all," Sam Gault said, his calloused feet stewing in a basin of water.

But for Jimmy Wright the times were exciting beyond every dream he ever had. He knew that William was carefully drawing all his troops into order. He was a serious monarch who planned everything carefully. On 18th June more reinforcements arrived from Hoylake in England, bringing up the strength of William's army. Belfast now teemed with soldiers from every country in Europe. Quartermasters spent wearing hours under the hot sun organising the munition waggons, the food for the troops, the tents and the field kitchens. Tents had been pitched in the fields around Belfast and the population of the town had doubled in two days. The taverns and the inns were filled with soldiers waiting for orders from their commanders.

Sam Gault had fifed through the taverns but he had collected only a few meagre coins. The soldiers were more interested in spending their money on drink than in listening to music.

"I'll have to wait for peace to return before I can turn a tune to money," he complained when he arrived at the hay barn in which they were billeted after three hours of worthless toil.

Everywhere men spoke confidently of victory. Rumours filtered through from the commanders of the army. Some believed that James had already left Ireland. Others believed that half his army had deserted him and fled to the woods and that he had drummed raw recruits into service. They marched with scythes and cudgels. But most important of all the spies said that William's artillery was better, more numerous, and that his gunners were the best in Europe. They had good judgement and knew where to plant a gun on the day of battle. On a slope outside the city they practised the art of gunnery with several raw recruits. The thunder of the explosions shook the ground beneath the feet of the horses. It was not a fruitless exercise to impress the soldiers. William wished to accustom the horses to the thunderous sound of battle. Nothing must be left to foolish chance.

William knew that most of the army would follow his general command. However, there was one regiment which lived by its own code. They were the guerilla forces from Enniskillen. They were rough riders, dressed in home-made leather clothes, stained from service and hard use. Their horses looked more like half starved nags barely fit to draw a plough. They were led by Colonel William Wolseley Gustavus Hamilton. They refused to take orders from any of William's commanders. They preferred to wage their own war. It was secretive and sudden. They never engaged in open combat. Instead, they chose their time and their terrain. They would sweep suddenly into a camp at evening time when soldiers were resting after a day's march, bear down upon them, make a quick kill and disappear again into the woods. They always moved at the edge of a retreating army. The struck at its weak flank like wolves following a herd. They did not fight for honour and they were not interested in William's discipline or his views. They were farmers and landowners who wished to protect their recently acquired land. This alone made them the fiercest of all William's forces. Sam Gault had played for some of them in a tavern but they had thrown him on to the street. They were dour-faced men who drank dourly.

"Small, mean farmers, tight with their money. They delay over their drinks, sucking the worth out of the ale," Sam Gault had complained to Jimmy Wright.

They spent a week in Belfast and soon they became acquainted with the regiments and their uniforms. And they became acquainted with the great commanders who passed imperiously through the town and had little truck with the common soldiers.

"This army is getting restless, Jimmy," Sam Gault told him one evening when he returned to the hayshed which had been their home for five days. By some means or other, he had acquired two pounds of bread and a roast chicken. These he took from sacking and laid on a plank. "Some of the Danish troops talk of mutiny. They want their pay in advance. Right trouble there for William."

Sam Gault ate his food with relish, picking neatly at the bones. He suggested that they keep the remainder for the next day.

"And now I sleep," he told Jimmy. "I feel satisfied and replete and no thanks to William of Orange."

He was about to lock his hands over his distended stomach when the bugle sounded. It was the call to arms.

"This is it. This is what I feared. I heard rumours among other things. I declare we are going to war," Sam Gault said. He took his fife and Jimmy took his drum and they rushed to their regiment. Already the soldiers were on the parade grounds. Sam Gault and Jimmy took their position before the long line of soldiers. A cavalry officer rode down past them and looked carefully at the order of men.

His statement was brief.

"Tomorrow we march towards Dublin. James is already falling back from the town of Dundalk. Sleep well tonight. King William sends you his best regards. Every regiment will receive an extra ration of wine. Long live William of Orange," he called.

"Long live William of Orange," they called back. They held their formation while the officer rode out of sight. Then they broke rank like rabble and rushed to the storehouse for wine. Sam Gault was last to reach the storehouse where the wine rested in large wooden tuns. While the soldiers in some disarray called for their wine and banged their pewter mugs against the wall, Sam Gault had whipped around to the back of the building. There he discovered a back entrance. He pushed the door aside and made his way into the storehouse. It was a large barn, filled with the dry smell of hay dust. The quartermaster stood anxiously at the door, unwilling to draw the oak beam against the pounding fists.

"Sam Gault reporting for duty," Sam Gault said smartly.

"What duty?" the anxious quartermaster asked.

"The duty to dispense wine," he said.

"Very well, very well," the quartermaster said. "Bang the bung from the barrel when I give orders."

"Certainly sir. Willing, ready and able," he told him, taking a mallet in hand.

The quartermaster opened the door anxiously. The soldiers rushed in and stood around the enormous cask.

"Order, order," Sam Gault called, conscious of his important position.

"We demand our wine. We demand our wine, Sam Gault," the soldiers cried out, banging their pewter tankards against the barrels. Sam banged in the bung, and red wine, like blood from a vein, gushed forward into the first pewter mug. Sam staunched the flow with a plug.

"Next," he said, as he unstopped the hole. Some order descended on the place and the men formed into a rotating circle, drinking their wine as they moved forward for more. Finally they were all given triple rations and sat along the wall. Sam Gault drew wine from a bucket he had conveniently set beside one of the tuns. He enjoyed its dark flavour. It was free and in limitless supply.

His mind was as yet not fuddled. He listened to the soldiers' talk. They were certain that a battle would take place and they mentioned a river called the Boyne. They believed that James would make his stand on the south side.

"William wants a rapid battle. He is not going to dally a winter in Ireland like old Count Schomberg. There is a coldness between them and the old count is ill-used and not in the council."

"And how are you intimate with what passes in the central councils," a soldier asked sharply. "Has William called on the foot soldier for advice?"

"No. But I have heard James Douglas and Percy French in conversation. And I know that tomorrow we march in four divisions south."

"And are we before or aft?" the soldier asked.

"Somewhere in the middle."

"Good. It suits me well to be in the middle."

They were now sitting on the great barn floor, a little drunk and sleepy. It was warm in the barn and filled with the half light of evening. A heavy shaft of sunshine poured through the wide door. Suddenly, a figure in a buff-coloured military coat with an orange sash and a cavalry sword in its scabbard appeared. He wore black leather bucket-style boots and a elegant hat with a coloured plume.

"Serving wine, Sam Gault?" William of Orange said. "Why, you serve my troops well. And have you not a flagon of wine for your King?"

"Yes, Your Majesty," Sam Gault said and rushed forward to where a pewter flagon had been left on a wooden ledge. He quickly dipped the flagon in the bucket and handed it to the King.

"To your health, Sam Gault, and to all our troops," he said, turning to the amazed soldiers who were now sheepishly standing by the wall.

"To his majesty, rightful King of England," they all called. The King took a small sip of the common wine, which must have been sharp on his tongue, handed it Sam Gault and left the storehouse.

They looked at Sam Gault in amazement. He nonchalantly sipped the King's wine

"How did the King know your name, Sam Gault?" one of the soldiers asked.

"We are old friends. Old friends. I knew him in the European wars. Often asked me for advice. He always said, 'Now, Sam, you are a Carrickfergus man. What do your think of our position?' And I would give an honest Carrickfergus man's opinion. More often than not he took my advice. And if William is on the throne of England today it's because he was well advised by Sam Gault," Sam Gault told them, his imagination now running free.

"You are a plain liar, Sam Gault, drunk and given to exaggeration," one of them said, but others had seen the familiarity and wondered.

Sam was very drunk when he left the great barn. He clung to the pewter mug from which the King had supped. He would never part with it as long as he lived.

"You are drunk," Jimmy Wright told him when he reached the hay barn. "How can you expect to drum soldiers forward if your head is reeling?"

But Sam would not listen.

"You see this tankard," he said "Well,

William of Orange and Sam Gault supped out of it this very day. Why, he remembered my name. Called me Sam Gault."

"You are drunk."

"No I'm not. The King remembered my name."

"And you can barely remember your own. So go to sleep."

Holding his tankard, Sam turned towards the barn wall and was soon asleep. For a small light man he snored loudly. Jimmy looked at the frail figure. If anybody could survive the ravages of war or live off a desolate countryside it was Sam Gault.

Jimmy Wright furled his body about his drum and fell asleep.

4

Retreat to the Boyne

atthew Desmond knew well the landscape through which the army of James now retreated from Ardee. He had passed its rolling fields during other summers when cattle grazed calmly in lush pastures. He had his own dreams then of a landscape firm, settled and at peace. Now, everywhere he looked there was confusion. As the vast army retreated they left behind smoking black columns, ascending into a blue sky. Nothing would be left on the landscape to sustain William and his army, not beast nor grain nor blade, though he had pleaded with one of James's advisers to leave the countryside at peace and not to stir up people against their cause.

Matthew Desmond had been seven days camped before Dundalk. It had given him plenty of time to examine their situation thoroughly. He had many misgivings about their position and the army. However, he had not spoken to his sons concerning his doubts. Each morning they were out and about the large camp meeting young cavalry soldiers, going through the exercises of war and sitting to dine at evening with their companions. Many of them had brought their silver plate with them and ate lavishly while the poorer soldiers starved. He preferred to eat frugally with the men under his command.

"Let us ride through our positions," Matthew Desmond told a fellow officer one evening. "I wish to examine our strength. We have now been here for seven days, waiting for William to advance towards us. Our positions are scattered and weak and thrown across too large a front. We must retreat to a line of defence that will give us the advantage. James should now move towards the Boyne."

By now spies had brought news of William's forces from the north. Day after day deserters found their way into the camp, willing to sell their secrets for a keg of ale. It was evident that William was strong in every section of his army, particularly in his artillery. He had fifty pieces at his command and some of the best gunners in Europe in charge of the heavy cannon.

As they passed across the camp the weakness of James's army was obvious to Matthew's seasoned eye. In one particular quarter they found men with pointed staves practising against a stuffed bag of hay. They were awkward and rough and had not been tested under fire. A massive cavalry charge would rout them and they could bring confusion to a battlefield. In another quarter men were armed only with scythes and elsewhere they discovered soldiers who were expecting arms.

"Louts and green recruits," Matthew Desmond remarked severely. "Do you think that they will stand up to cannon fire or tested troops? They are a useless burden to carry with us. They should be discharged."

At the outer edge of the army lurked the scavengers. They were the human ravens of the battlefields. They were the outcasts of society who robbed the bodies of the dead after battle when the night had fallen. They were the creatures of darkness and death. Their white eyes in dark and dirty faces watched and waited from behind ditches.

Frequently they were chased from the edge of the camp. They disappeared into the woods like scattered birds. But they crept back later and kept up their vigil.

Matthew Desmond found the tested troops in good heart. They were camped closer to the town and each battalion was well organised. Many of the soldiers played cards or dice. Some just polished their weapons out of habit. Their swords, unlike those of the new recruits, were strong and flexible and would not snap in combat.

They moved to the north of the city. Then a company of soldiers suddenly came towards them. They had captured two officers at Moyra Pass.

"Perhaps they can give us better information than we have received from the deserters," Matthew Desmond told his companion. They followed the soldiers to the town where they had set up a prison. The captives were separated and then each one was questioned. The information they gave the officers differed only in slight details from that already received:

William's army was now fully equipped with arms but rations would last only for a week. They hoped to live off the land as they passed through. All the regiments were in quarters and ready to march. These consisted of professional troops. They had been hardened on the battlefields of Europe. They were well-armed and well-clothed and their pay had been brought up to date. Matthew Desmond's worst fears were realised. William's army outnumbered the Jacobite troops by ten thousand men.

"This information must be immediately brought to King James and his commanders. I think the final decision will rest on this latest news," Matthew Desmond told them. He knew now that they would lose the battle.

James was having a meal in his tent when Matthew Desmond asked permission to enter. The king, sipping a goblet of wine, bade him sit down. He indicated to his servant to bring Matthew Desmond some wine but Matthew modestly refused. The tent was lavishly set out and it was difficult to imagine that they were very close to a great battle. James wore a brown periwig which fell in luxurious ringlets on his shoulders. He was dressed in a blue satin coat with gold buttons. Fine lace on his cuffs added to an air of elegance which was foreign to a battlefield.

"Well, Matthew Desmond, what serious

news do you carry to me?" he asked.

"We have captured two cavalry soldiers in the Moyra Pass. We have questioned them rigorously. They confirm what we already knew. William is almost ready to march. His troops outnumber ours by ten thousand and they have all been well tested in battles," he said firmly.

James sipped his wine and spoke:

"And so our worst fears are confirmed. We have no option but to retreat. If we choose to fight at Dundalk then we have little advantage. It is too open and provides no cover. As I stated in Dublin, we will withdraw to the Boyne."

"Could I suggest that we move along the south side of the river towards Connaught? It is better to avoid an engagement. William cannot afford to have a protracted war."

"That would give him a free passage to Dublin. No, Dublin must be defended. If we take up a position behind the Shannon we throw ourselves into a dungeon. I have taken the decision. I will call a council of war. We must command an orderly retreat."

Matthew Desmond left the king's tent and returned to his squadron. It was now late evening. From the camp-fires smoke ascended slowly towards the sky. He could smell meat roasting over spits. It was still warm and men had cast aside their arms. Matthew Desmond knew that the battle would be fought under a hot sky. Men's tongues would parch and harden from lack of water and the corpses would have to be buried rapidly.

However, when he sat down to write to his wife he did not mention any of his fears. He described the seven days he had spent before Dundalk and the preparations they were making for an engagement. He wrote of his meeting with King James. He told her that the army was in good heart and that their sons kept well. He signed the letter, and then sealed it with his ring. His personal servant took the letter and set out for Dublin.

That night the decision was taken by James that they would retreat. Most of his generals agreed with the plan. However, many were doubtful as to the wisdom of doing battle with William. Much later Sarsfield and many others sat about the camp-fires and considered their positions. Many believed that they should steal out of the camp with their troops. They owed only doubtful allegiance to James. He was not interested in their aspirations. He was not interested in Ireland. He wished only to be restored to the throne of England.

"And remember, James was sent by Louis of France to draw William from England. At this present moment the southern coast of England is lightly guarded. They all play at games. We are the pawns on the chess-board of war, not even the knights," Sarsfield told his friends.

"We cannot desert now. Honour demands that we stay and see the thing out to the bitter end," a young officer replied.

"Yes, as gentlemen we cannot desert this cause," another advised.

"Had we a different king I would feel that we stood some chance," Sarsfield told them. "But I think it is ill-advised to engage in battle. We have only one advantage and that is time. William cannot afford this valuable commodity. We can. Do not talk to me of honour while we bury our dead."

"And do you agree with his policy of burning the towns and the food supplies as we retreat?" one asked.

"I would if it were to prolong the war. I would even poison the wells. I would starve William. And when his soldiers were sick and weak and fevered I would attack."

"But that is not war."

"That is war," he replied firmly.

All night in small conclaves men discussed the strategy of war. For the most part they were tired of long calm days sitting about waiting for some small incident to enliven their lives. The battle energy was growing in them.

Next morning the retreat from Dundalk was sounded. Men gathered in their companies and at a drum tuck they began to move slowly in a long straggling cavalcade. It took many hours to pass through the countryside towards Ardee. And behind them they left only burned ruins and empty barns. Cattle were driven forward in great confused herds. And everywhere there was dry dust hanging on the warm air as the army marched onwards.

Two days they rested at Ardee. During this time the troops plundered the houses and killed some of the inhabitants. Many fled from the town and took refuge in the countryside, waiting for the plague to pass. When the army moved out they left behind empty streets where only dogs dared to move. All food that could not be carried by the army was destroyed.

Two days later they finally reached a favourable position beyond the arm of the Boyne, a river sacred in Irish mythology. It was a good position on a slope of a hill facing north. Here they set up positions on 30 June. They knew that William was now on the march and some miles behind. In fact they had seen the clouds of smoke billowing up in the distance. It was obvious that he would now pitch his tents on the northern hills above the river.

On the evening of the 30 June young John Desmond watched a messenger ride furiously up the drive to the castle. He carried a letter from his father. It was delivered to his mother who went to her room to read it. But John Desmond was more interested in the messenger. He followed him down to the kitchen. And there while the messenger ate his supper, John Desmond learned more than he would have from his father's letter. He was certain now that a battle would take place at the Boyne. He supressed his excitement. But that night, when his mother believed he was in bed, he slipped out of the castle to the stables. He was dressed in his uniform and had his sword by his side.

There was summer light in the sky as he made his way through the estate towards the Drogheda road. He would be in Drogheda in six hours and in time for the battle.

5

Going to War

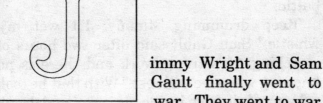

immy Wright and Sam Gault finally went to war. They went to war on a summer's morning. It was cool when they rose from their sleep and the water which they splashed on their faces was soft. After a brisk meal they went to the square and took up their positions before a battalion of soldiers dressed in blue coats and white breeches. At a signal Jimmy Wright and Sam Gault started on their marching tune. They stepped forward and moved out of the square. Each company in turn swung in behind them. They led the soldiers down through the town. Soon the houses fell away behind them and they were in open country. It grew warmer. Jimmy Wright felt sweat pour down his forehead. He could not wipe it away. He must drum the men forward until they got the order to halt.

And while this small part of the army marched forward towards Dundalk, other sections were following other orders. Under King William, some thirty five thousand men were on the march, across a wide spread of land Nothing could now prevent the final battle.

"Keep drumming, Jimmy. I'll wet my whistle," Sam Gault said after two hours of marching. "It's tiring work and there is no knowing when we will rest." With that he took a flagon of ale from inside his jacket and drank from it as he marched forward. His pewter tankard swung from his belt, to be used only on great occasions.

And just then a captain rode by. He saw Sam Gault with the bottle to his lips. He kicked it from his hand. It went spinning onto the grass and poured freely into the dry earth.

"I'll have you horse-whipped if I catch you drinking on the march. Play for the men. Put them in good cheer," he roared and would have brought the flat of his sword down on Sam Gault's back had he not quickly pulled out his fife and begun to play.

"Where is your friend King William when you most need him, Sam Gault?" one of the soldiers called. There was general laughter in the long ranks. Then they fell silent and continued the march.

The sun was hot and high when they reached their first rest position. The soldiers fell out on orders. They were close to a stream. They rushed forward and lay flat on their stomachs and cupped the water into their mouths with their hands. Then they stretched out on the grass and tried to rest.

When Sam Gault had slaked his thirst, he took off his boots and plunged his boiled feet in the stream.

"This is heaven. This is heaven," he told Jimmy Wright.

"Don't poison the stream, Sam," a soldier called to him. Again they began to laugh. Jimmy Wright felt sorry for his friend. He knew that he was offended at their mocking.

"I'll remember their nasty remarks, faith I will, when it comes to the burial day. I have seen hearty, laughing lads go the way of all flesh. Let them laugh and have their joke. Sam Gault will have his day," he replied bitterly, now rubbing his sore feet.

"I'm not made for this, Jimmy. I have better uses for my time and music," Sam Gault complained.

"But we fight in a good cause. We fight for

William and his cause. The old enemy must be defeated," Jimmy answered.

"You have been listening to those who would set daft notions in your head. It don't matter whether we are Protestant or Catholic, Jimmy lad. You and I will always be among the poor. Come King James or come King William none is going to make me Lord of Castlefergus."

"Men have been hanged, Sam Gault, for words like that," Jimmy Wright said seriously.

"I know, but who will hang Sam Gault. I own no land or possessions. 'Twould be a waste of a rope," he laughed.

"I fight in a good cause, Sam Gault, and I won't be stirred. The preacher warned me against you and so did others."

They had no time to continue the conversation. The captain rode by, calling out: "Up, you dogs. You did not join William's army to sleep. The enemy lies ahead. He must be routed. To your feet and on your way."

They men stirred from their pleasant positions on the grass and formed into line. One with enthusiasm and the other without enthusiasm, Jimmy Wright and Sam Gault began a marching tune. They marched through an empty village. The inhabitants had fled into the woods as they approached. Already they noted that the land was empty of cattle. No army could live off the countryside. The Jacobites had deprived the army of its food source.

As they marched further they noted that houses and hay reeks had been set on fire. They were charred masses that could give no comfort or shelter to anyone.

Jimmy Wright was not certain what was hanging from the tree. But as he approached he knew that it was a soldier. He was dressed in a red coat and a white trousers. Somebody had stolen his boots and his feet were bare, his toes blue. There was a tight cord about his broken neck. His head had fallen to one side and his tongue was long and loose. His eyes were wide and vacant.

"A Frenchman by the look of him," a soldier behind Jimmy remarked, "and a spy, no doubt."

"And there will be more evil fruit from the hanging trees along the way," his companion said.

"Well it is certain that we are marching in the right direction," came the laughing remark.

It was Jimmy Wright's first introduction to war. He felt for a moment he was going to fall out and vomit. But he held control of himself and marched forward.

Finally, after six hours of marching with only a short break, they reached Loughbrickland. The small village was already occupied by many regiments. They pitched their tents about the fields and soon smoke was ascending from camp-fires. Men could now relax after the weary march and smoke tobacco and talk. They would eat and talk again later. Their conversation always centred around battles which they had fought in Europe. They were hardened soldiers and could march many long miles without complaint and lie in open fields in cold rain or in hot, baking weather.

The chief news concerned the retreat of James's army. He had retreated from Dundalk leaving the town intact, and was now camped at Ardee. It meant that the battle would not now take place in June. The soldiers could therefore relax about the camp-fires.

"It gives them another day to live," Sam Gault remarked sourly. He was in a bad mood. His feet hurt. He had no ready food available. A captain had kicked his flagon of beer from

his hand and he had suffered insults from the
common soldier. He took out his fife and began
to play a quiet, sad tune.

"I never heard you play that before, Sam."

"I never had cause to."

"And where did your learn it?"

"From a blind Irish harper."

"I thought that you had no truck with the
Irish."

"I may have little time for them but I like
their music."

"That doesn't make sense."

"There is a lot that doesn't make sense in
this world and nothing makes sense on a
battlefield."

When he had satisfied some sadness within
him, his anger and confidence returned. He
took out his dice and went off to win his supper. Jimmy Wright followed him. They walked
to the very centre of the encampment where
the professional troops had set up their
quarters. They were better clad and better fed
than the new recruits. Some had set up tables
outside their tents and were drinking ale and
eating roast meat from pewter plates.

"A dice for a dinner. A dice for a dinner,"
Sam Gault called to the soldiers who were
enjoying their leisurely meal.

"And what will you wager, yokel?" someone asked.

"A significant ring. A ring of quality. A royal ring." And from his pocket he took out a fine ring of gold and crystal. He placed it on the table and the soldiers examined it with care. It was a genuine and valuable ring.

"And from whom did you steal this precious ring?" one of them asked.

"I received it from a patron, my good sir. Now I have fallen upon hard times so I wager it against a good supper."

"Done," they said. "Three tosses of the dice for a diamond or a dinner."

"Very well, my good sirs," he said and cast the dice across the table. It fell five upward.

They tried three times against him, yet every time he tossed, the dice fell in his favour.

They tested it for bias and tested it again and again to see if they could discover some fault in it. In the end they handed him back his ring and a good dinner with a large bottle of wine. This he ate in their presence, using his fork expertly and not like a common soldier. He passed Jimmy Wright a good meaty bone and directed him to chew upon it. He belched contentedly when he was finished.

He handed back the pewter plate and returned to his former position on the edge of the camp.

"You toss the dice very well, Sam Gault," Jimmy Wright told him.

"I toss two dice. You see I have practised sleight-of-hand for many years. Look." And with that he drew a dice from Jimmy Wright's nose. Then he drew one from his eye. And when he opened his hands the dice had disappeared.

"Then you are an imposter," Jimmy Wright said.

"Not an imposter. I am a magician. I make dice disappear and dinners appear. These soldiers did not miss a dinner. They are British troops, William's own men, and they eat well. Now I shall drink good French wine and forget about this battle."

He drew off the cork with a dagger and set down to drink slowly, drawing pleasure from every mouthful. Then he began to sing some ballads he had composed himself, "during hours of mystical vision," he told Jimmy Wright.

Much later he fell asleep under a cart of hay that had been positioned close by.

Next morning they moved out early. Men

knew that each day the battle drew closer.
They were more serious now. Everywhere
they could see the blackened scars left by
James's army. Houses were burned to the
ground, crops reduced to white ash. The fields
were empty of cattle. Newry was an empty
shell. Corpses, swollen and fetid, lay unburied
in the streets. A few old people, shaken and
confused by the presence of war, wandered
aimlessly from darkened door to darkened
door.

That evening, after a forced march, part of
the army reached Dundalk. The town had
been deserted by James's forces and already
news had been carried to the camp that James
had moved further south and crossed the
Boyne. It was evident to the seasoned soldiers
that the battle would take place at this river.

By this time Jimmy Wright was tired from
marching. The vast numbers of troops and the
continual movement of men and animals
confused him. He no longer knew where he
was. He could not forget the bodies he had
seen hanging from the branches of the trees.
And just as he was about to settle in for the
evening they was confused shouting from a
wood nearby. A young boy was dragged into
the camp. He was about twelve years of age. A

soldier pulled him forward by the hair and threw him in front of his captain.

"He tried to lure us into an ambush a week ago. His face is familiar to me."

The captain took his sword and held it at the young boy's neck.

"Confess all you know. Is all this true?"

"Yes. I did it in a good cause. I hate you and all you stand for. You took my father's land and reduced us to poverty. I do not fear your sword," he said viciously.

"He has sealed his own fate. Hang him," the captain ordered. The men instantly tied his hands and threw a rope across the branch of a tree. They drew up a horse-cart and placed him upon it. Then they beat the animal forward. The boy's neck was instantly broken. He hung limply from the tree. The men turned their backs on him and resumed their duties. They were now on battle ground and the normal laws no longer existed. Jimmy Wright was fascinated by the young boy who was now dead. Five minutes earlier he had been alive. Jimmy had not been so close to death before.

"Come away from this sight, Jimmy Wright. It does not suit you," Sam Gault told him.

"I'm going to be sick, Sam," he said and with that he vomited on to the ground.

Sam took him by the arm and led him away.

"I should never have fifed for William. We should still be in in Carrickfergus if things were half right. But there is no getting out of it now. If we desert we will be hanged, so we have no choice but to go forward."

Jimmy Wright went forward at every command. He was now confused and had lost his keen interest in the army. He did not know where he was going. He followed the line of soldiers ahead of him, drumming the marching step.

On the evening of 30 June, at the end of a long hot summer's day, both Jimmy White and Sam Gault found themselves on Tullyallen Hill above the river Boyne. On a slope beyond the river lay James's army, set out in formation and ready to do battle.

6

The Eve of the Battle

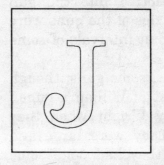immy Wright and
Sam Gault had felt
unimportant during the
last few days. Now as they gazed down upon
the battlefield they felt completely
insignificant. As Sam Gault could only count
to ten on his fingers he had no way of knowing
that the strength of King William's army
stood at thirty-five thousand men, give or take
a few, and King James's at about twenty-five
thousand. Neither had he any way of knowing
that King James stood little chance in the
battle.

They stood on the summit of the hill and
looked about them. It was a long slow summer
evening. They sun was sinking in the west and
throwing muted gold colour on the hills. The
great cannon that had barked out at each
other on either side had fallen silent at eight

o'clock and the gunners had retired to a stream to bathe. The barrels of powder had been taken to a safe distance behind the lines and the great balls slotted into the gun carriage trails. The nozzles of the guns were cooling now. They stood at intervals of some three hundred yards.

"These are some guns, some guns, though they be not the greatest of William's guns," Sam Gault told Jimmy Wright when they stood beneath them. They were large and gleaming and already they had done some damage during the day to the less accurate guns of James II. From their dangerous position beside the guns they could see the grey camps of James II set out in two long lines from the small village of Oldbright to Rathmullen. Here and there standards were caught by an easy breeze and showed their colours and their markings. Smoke was passing up into the evening sky from the camp-fires. Men were preparing for the night. Many were brushing down their horses with slow strokes as they would before a great parade. Others polished their weapons or sat in circles gambling, trying to dispel their fears.

Sam Gault looked at the sky. He did not like

this inland scene, with its woods and river. Inland it baked and the earth became too hot. There was too much land and he could not take his bearings from Castlefergus castle. He wished he were in Carrickfergus, close to the cooling sea.

"It is not the season for a battle," he told Jimmy Wright. "It be too hot and the days are too long. Spring or autumn yes, but not high summer. The peace of the countryside should not be broken by cannon crack or the thunder of horses."

A shot rang out from the far shore. The ball ricocheted from the gun barrel above them. They could see a puff of smoke ascending from the entrenchments opposite them. Sam Gault cut short his talk. He turned on his heels, ran up the hill and down the dip and sat on the grass exhausted.

"That were a near one, Jimmy Wright. I strongly wonder why I ever got caught up in this war which is not of my making and has no concern for me. My life is of as much worth to me as William's is to him."

"You are a coward, Sam Gault. Others look forward to the battle. God is on our side," Jimmy told him

"Were you talking to God?" Sam asked

querulously

"No. But I've heard the soldiers and the captains talk among themselves. They believe in it firmly."

"And over in the camp of James there are soldiers preparing for battle believing that God is on their side. Well, I'll tell you something, Jimmy Wright—God is on the side of Sam Gault and he has been telling me since I got deeper and deeper into this mess that I made a mistake when I took the first step towards the Boyne. I have a good mind to escape when night falls."

"And be hanged?"

"Ah," he said, from the comfort of the covert. He had not contemplated flight before. Now as the sun sank deeper and the shadows in the forests lengthened, it became a more attractive idea. Once into the woods he could move freely north. He could bandage a leg, shape a crutch and walk the road as a wounded soldier. However, he knew that if he were discovered deserting he could be hanged.

He reflected seriously on all these matters.

Meanwhile at the ruined monastery of Mellifont some miles to the rear, William was drawing up his final plans for the battle. He would not throw all his army across the Boyne river. Instead he would divide it. Under cover of night Count Meinhard Schomberg and General Douglas would move south-east, divide, and cross the river at several points. Here they could set up a second front. They would attack James's army from two directions.

"I'm entitled to rum," Sam Gault said, stirring from his reverie. "Whatever else happens I'm entitled to rum and I'll have my rum from King William's flagon."

He stirred himself from his position, climbed up the hill and peered over cautiously. He looked once more at the spread of tents and men across the hill of Donore. If fortune favoured him he would be far from the battle next day. He now lacked all taste for war.

He turned and marched straight into the the camp of the Dutch Blue Guards. They were serious men and talked in a guttural language. They sat in small groups beside their tents and threw dice on to a square canvas. They watched the turn of the dice seriously, nodding their heads at victory and defeat. He found their quartermaster at the rum cask.

"Fifer Sam Gault, to lead great Dutch Blue Guards," he said in a piteous Dutch accent and he took out his fife and played on it.

"Vhat you whisler vant?" the Dutch quartermaster asked.

"Rum ration," he said and took out his tankard.

"You no fool me. You go jump in the Voine," the Dutchman said and went to draw his sword.

"Retreat." Sam Gault said and he beat a retreat from the camp. He tried to play the same trick on the Huguenot regiment. But they were not interested in drink or dice. To them they were about to take part in a sacred battle. They would settle old scores with Louis XIV who had banished them from France. For these serious and pious men it was not an Irish battle. It was a French battle fought on Irish soil.

"Dull dogs," Sam Gault commented to Jimmy Wright who had followed him closely. "I've come half way across the camp and not a drop of rum has wet my tongue. I'm entitled to rations."

Jimmy Wright admired him for many of his qualities. He knew something about everything and nothing much about anything and he had been almost everywhere in Europe fifing and burying the battle dead. But he had no great love for any cause outside of himself. He was argumentative, itchy to be on the move and he drank too much. The parson in Carrickfergus had told Jimmy Wright that drink was a scourge and an abomination. This Jimmy believed as he believed in the good cause he was now engaged in. Despite his fears, he would lead a regiment into battle, down the slope and into the river and out onto the enemy lines.

"I'll try the English," Sam Gault said eventually when he arrived at the English camp. "I trust the English."

He was fortunate. They needed a fifer and a drummer and they needed some entertainment before the battle. It was one of these situations in which Sam Gault was most happy. Not only did he play on his fife but he did a small dance for the soldiers and even juggled some shot for them. All the time Jimmy Wright kept rhythm by the tuck of his drum. He had been well trained by Sam Gault and could vary his speed and his sound to the needs of the occasion.

Much later when it was almost dark, Sam Gault began to miss notes on his fife and balls of shot in his juggling. He had drunk deeply and it was time to rest.

As they settled in under a large baggage truck Sam Gault's mind turned to desertion. He would travel England juggling and playing the fife. He would bring Jimmy Wright with him. They would travel to the South of England where it was warm. Perhaps they would travel to France where it was warmer still. They would avoid Italy. The Pope lived somewhere in Italy and he was afraid of the Pope. They argued about desertion under the baggage cart. This was the last chance they had. If they fell asleep they would rise only to the trumpet for battle.

"I'll not go, Sam Gault. I'll stand and fight," Jimmy Wright told him with finality.

Sam Gault waited until the young drummer was asleep. There was general silence about the camp and a friendly darkness. Here and there a camp-fire burned, with soldiers hooped over the intimate flames. They spoke only in whispers. He knew that there would be sentries posted about the camp. He must be careful as he went. He passed out of the English camp and moved north, keeping a firm eye on the north star. He passed sleeping men like a cautious cat. He could see the woods, massed and half luminous to the north. The moon was in his favour. He passed across the final open patch of ground. A horse whinnied for a moment. With a quick dash he was in the wood. He had escaped. And then there was a rough arm about him, a dagger to his throat. His small body was lifted from the ground and he was dragged back into the clearing and to a circle of camp-fire.

"I've caught a spy, me lads," an Enniskillener told his companions as he threw Same Gault on the ground. "He came to spy on us and carry news of our position back to James."

"I'm a good Protestant. Sure you saw me fife the army to the Boyne," he told them, his small hands spread out as he moved about the circle and tried to plead his position with men who knew the woods and the wild places better than anyone else in the army.

"If you are not a spy then you are a deserter or a scavenger," they told him. "You are either with us or against us. You seem to be against us."

They were taunting him. He felt like a small animal stalked by a circle of rough dogs.

"I've always been for our cause. I've torn pages from the Catholic Bible in protest. I have sworn allegiance to the Protestant cause," he cried. Fear was tightening in his throat. He could not escape. He looked at the passionless eyes of the men. He knew their reputation.

"Hang him," one Enniskillener called out. "He is a burden to us and to the army. He was born to swing. He's a twister."

"I'm King William's friend. Honestly I am," he called in one desperate effort.

"William's friend. William's friend," they called to each other in laughter.

"And I suppose you know King James?" someone asked.

"No, I only know King William. We are friends," he cried out. "I'm a fifer. I will fife for you tomorrow."

"We have no truck with drums or fifes," one of the men said. "We move to the music of swords. Hang him and be done with it."

Without ceremony or blessing they drew Sam Gault to a nearby tree. They felt some pleasure in hurting this small eel-like man. They put a noose around his neck and hoisted him on horse-back. Sam Gault was too frightened to cry out. He would die on the edge of an army camp on the eve of a famous battle.

At Mellifont the council of war broke up before final darkness. The battle plan had been decided upon. The army would divide.

The attack would be from two directions. At two o'clock that night the right wing of William's army would move west under cover of darkness, ford the river Boyne and be in position for the battle. It would begin at 10.30 when the tidal river would be at its lowest.

And now William could not sleep. He could never sleep on the eve of a battle. Besides, his arm pained him. The evening before, while surveying they opposing lines, he had received a wound from an enemy cannon. It had taken a piece of his coat and torn the skin and flesh of his arm.

He ordered his horse and some torches. As darkness fell he moved through the camp. Despite his bad health, his faulty English and his cold demeanour, the soldiers respected his presence. He always visited the camps before battle. Quietly he moved from place to place, speaking to the captains and the men. He spoke of the battle and told them that victory was already secure. Men cheered quietly as he passed out of their section attended by six torchbearers.

"The King is coming. The King is coming," one of the Enniskilleners called to his companions who were about to hang Sam Gault. They abandoned the small figure and

rushed forward to greet King William. Sam
Gault hoped that the horse would not rush
forward in the excitement. The King rode into
the light of the camp-fire. Men gathered about
him and pledged their allegiance. His eyes
caught the figure of Sam Gault. He urged his
horse forward. The circle of torches moved
with him.

"Sam Gault, I declare," King William said.
"I see, Sam, that you have acquired a horse
and a hempen collar. Has my good friend
deserted me when I need him most?"

"A grave mistake, Your Majesty. A
miscarriage of justice. A call of nature brought
me to the wood, where I was captured and
tried without court. I have pledged myself to
lead your best soldiers into battle," he said in a
half choked voice.

"Sam Gault, I hope you tell your King no lies
or half-lies. You will gain a reprieve but
tomorrow you lead the troops across the river.
I shall be watching with my eye-glass. Cut my
good friend down and let him return to his
regiment."

The Enniskilleners were amazed at the
familiarity between King and fifer. They took
Sam Gault from the horse and removed the
hempen rope. His rubbed his neck with his

fingers. He could feel the rope print. He had been lucky.

"Good night, Your Majesty, and a good day to you tomorrow," he said.

"And a good day to you, Sam Gault. We expect every man to do his duty," the King told him.

With that Sam Gault escaped from the circle of light and from notice. He made his way back to the English camp and crept under the baggage cart. Reluctantly, he would now have to take part in the battle.

* * * * *

John Desmond looked at the luminous stars in the night sky and at the bright moon. He urged his horse forward along the dust road. The horse was sure-footed and kept up a good speed. He passed through the black mass of small deserted villages. The inhabitants had fled. He was aware only of the sound of the horses' hooves, the jangle of harness, the forced breath of the animal. He had journeyed this road before to friends in Drogheda and could take easy bearings from the countryside bathed in the light of the moon. Warm peace lay on the ghostly landscape, a grey mist spread over the fields and about the small valleys.

He was anxious to be with his brothers. In his imagination he saw himself riding forward into battle with his brothers and father. With swords drawn they would drive the enemy back across the Boyne. He would be with them for the great victory. It was late in the night when he reached the edge of the battlefield. He dismounted and led his horse through the vast settlement of tents. He could not find his father and his brothers. When he woke the soldiers, they cursed at him truculently and turned back into sleep. Finally he also decided to sleep. He was weary and tired after his journey. He lay down beside a heap of saddles, placed his head on some hay and fell asleep. His body grew cold and he awakened several times.

Somewhere in the middle of the camp James II was asleep. He had made the fatal decision that his army should take their stand at the Boyne. He felt that victory would not be given to him.

Matthew Desmond had argued with his sons after the final council of war. But they lacked his caution. They had the battle frenzy in their hearts and believed that with a gallant charge they could defeat William's best cavalry. They were as reckless as they were brave. Matthew Desmond, along with many battle-tested soldiers, had advised a long war. William must be held down in Ireland, while Louis XIV won victories in France. But men had divided minds over the battle.

Matthew Desmond could not sleep. He walked through the camp. His mind was anxious for the future. Only his young son would carry on the name if they died at the Boyne. He passed a young boy sleeping on the ground, barely noticing him in the darkness. He wondered whose son he was. He passed on. He could not sleep. His mind was in turmoil. The Catholic cause would not triumph. If the battle was lost then there would be more confiscations, more refugees. He was tired of battle. He wished for peace and time to tend his estates.

There was never final darkness that night. There was always the suggestion of some grey light in the sky.

While James's camp slept the enemy were making their way east. By morning they would have crossed the Boyne. Already the seeds of defeat were stirring in the night.

7

The Battle

hile Jimmy Wright and Sam Gault slept under a hay-cart, the right flank of the great army began to rouse itself out of a short sleep. A flat and magical mist covered the ground as the cavalrymen saddled their horses and drew themselves wearily onto their saddles. Count Meinhard Schomberg moved through the camp, drawing the foot soldiers and the cavalry into marching order. Then at his command they moved west towards the Mattock river. Here the army split. One wing moved towards Slane. The greatest number of men, however, marched between the mounds of Knowth and Newgrange towards Rosnaree, where they intended to ford the river at a shallow place.

While Jimmy Wright and Sam Gault continued to sleep, the sun rose into a cloudless sky. It banished the mist and began to warm the earth even at that early hour. It was too pleasant a morning to begin a battle. They would have continued to sleep had not the drums for battle sounded. Everywhere they were surrounded by cavalry and dragoons. They grabbed their instruments and stood, confused, on Tullyallen hill.

"I'm beginning to lose the taste for battle, Sam," Jimmy Wright said as the huge guns began to pound savagely. The thunder rang in his ear and he felt small and insignificant.

"I never had such a taste. I'm a coward," Sam replied firmly.

"Sam, I think I'm becoming a coward. I enjoyed drumming the army to battle but now that we're here it's a different matter."

"Fife and drums for the Dutch Blue Guards," a quartermaster called. "Hurry to right position. They are ready to move forward."

"We have no orders to play for the Dutch Blue Guards," Sam said boldly. The quartermaster took out his pistol and directed it at his head.

"Will you argue with my pistol?" he called.

"I'll not argue."

"Then hasten into position."

They joined other fifers and drummers on the crest of the hill. It sloped towards the Boyne which was now at a low level. On the opposite slope lay the Jacobite army, making no move.

"Play the Lillibulero and put heart into the Dutch Guards," the quartermaster ordered.

The drums sounded and the fifes took up the jaunty beat. The fifers and drummers moved forward and downwards, Sam beside Jimmy.

"Keep to the edge of the line so we can slip aside when the charge begins. And dive for cover when the shooting starts," Sam told him.

Behind them they could hear the excited breathing of horses, wide chest to wide chest. Forward they marched and downwards, the river bank growing nearer, the limpid water flowing past in the bright sunlight. Jimmy kept his eyes on the hedges and the breastworks on the far side of the river. They bristled with gun barrels. There was a menacing silence, punctuated by the pounding of the great guns.

And then they were at the river edge.

"Stand aside," Sam said, "and keep playing."

The fifers and drummers formed a line and the cavalry in rows of eight moved forward into the river. Their faces were eager for battle. No shots rang out from the Jacobite side. The fifers and drummers played them into the river. Each guard carried three grenades. These they would light and throw at the enemy when they reached the far side.

The battle suddenly began. A volley of fire tore into the lines of the Dutch Blue Guards. Some fell into the river but the others pressed on. And then they were across and attacking the Jacobite defences.

"Dive for cover now," Sam ordered and both of them dived on the ground. From a prone position they watched the war turn in William's favour. Despite a few bodies lying in the river most of the seasoned guards had made it to the far side. They pushed the enemy out of the small village of Oldbridge and secured it. Then with their position established, they reformed their ranks and waited for reinforcements.

"What should we do?" Sam asked.

"Withdraw. We've done our duty. We put heart into them and look at the fine victory they have achieved."

They rose from their position and marched up the hill of Tullyallen to a safe position. Here Sam, thinking that his work was done, intended to enjoy the rest of the day. They could survey the vast scene of the battle from their position. Both camps had become suddenly active. There was movement in all directions. On the sloping land to the south James's army was forming into divisions and regiments. Guns were speaking out against William's position but were without great effect.

The sun had risen in the sky and the day was growing warm. The morning coolness had disappeared and the ground was solid, the grass dry. The cavalry sounded like distant thunder on the hard earth. The attack by the Dutch Blue Guards had been only the beginning of the battle. Now William ordered the colonial regiments, the Enniskilleners and several others across the river. They marched forwards in a wide firm formation.

"Hurry. Hurry," Sam Gault called out and pounded his small hand on the ground. "Can't you see that James's cavalry will cut off the Guards?"

Jimmy Wright looked towards Donore Hill. At least a thousand men in battalions and squadrons advanced on the Dutch soldiers. But the Dutch regiment formed into hard square masses, bayonets firm on muskets. The great wave of cavalry could not break through the sharp defence of pointed steel. They drew away and reformed. Then they charged down upon the dour ranks and again the great wave broke on the wall of bayonets.

"They cannot carry the strain. They will break under a third attack," Sam Gault remarked from his safe position. By now the the cavalry squadrons and the regiments had entered the river, as James's cavalry bore down for a third time upon the Dutch Blue Guards. But as they did so the great mass of men were crowding on to the south bank of the river. The battle was now fought on a tangled and wide front. And everywhere it was was obvious that William's seasoned soldiers would win the day. Here and there Sam Gault observed brave sallies from the Jacobite cavalry but it was of little effect against the mass of men who forgot had now secured a sound footing at the base of Donore Hill.

"And look at old Schomberg," Sam Gault said, prodding Jimmy Wright in the ribs. "Look at him go."

He was now massing the centre, where the fighting was most intense. Men tangled with each other in hand to hand combat.

"What have we got here? What have we got here? Deserters?" a voice said behind them.

They looked up into the face of the quartermaster. "Think you have your day's work done? Not likely. The Danish Division will move off in fifteen minutes. They need music and they need music now."

He whipped out his pistol and pointed it at them. They rose from the ground and marched across Tullyallen Hill. They took up their position in front of the Danes. At a signal from the commander, Wurtemburg-Neustadt, Jimmy Wright, along with the other drummers, beat out the advance. By now the battle was raging furiously. Shot whistled about them as they advanced. Part of James's army was massing to meet them. They could never hope to ford the river.

Sam Gault feared for his life. The front was so wide that he could not move to one side. He watched nervously as they approached the river bank. He could see it stained with blood. He continued to play. Jimmy Wright could hear the clash of battle close by. Men screamed like animals as they fought in hand-to-hand combat. He watched men fall into the river and drown. And still they advanced. If they turned back they would be trampled upon.

"What will we do Sam?" Jimmy Wright cried.

"I hope God is on my side," Sam Gault replied. "Can you swim?"

"No."

"Neither can I."

And now they were on the very edge of the river. It seemed very wide and very deep. But men pushed on from behind. They could not stop now. Sam Gault and Jimmy Wright moved into the river which ran red with diluted blood. Behind them the whole army entered the river. The water grew deeper and Jimmy began to panic.

"Float the drum. Float the drum," Sam Gault called to him through the din. Jimmy Wright quickly unhooked the drum and placed it on the water. He moved forward. And then his feet could not feel the bottom. He began to panic. On the opposite side the Jacobites were beginning to advance to the bank of the river. They would surely be cut to pieces by gunfire. And then Jimmy Wright was truly out of his depth. The great river tugged at his body. The noise of the battle was all about him and a volley of lead shot cut up the water beside him.

"Sam. Sam," he screamed, his eyes wide and strained by terror. And then he felt Sam at his side. He put Jimmy's hands on the drum and held him close. Both floated downstream and to the edge of the advancing army. Now out of danger they floated onto the opposite bank. It was steep and no army would cross here. Sam found a sally bush in full leaf growing out from the bank. He drew Jimmy up on to its trunk. The young boy was wet and confused. His teeth chattered.

"I'm afraid, Sam. I do not want to die. I don't wish to be part of this battle," he mumbled.

"And so am I. So am I. Stay with Sam and both of us will live. I have nothing to gain from the battle. For me it is now all over."

"Are we safe Sam?"

"Jimmy, this tree trunk is the safest place there is, mark my words. I tell you no lie when I tell you that. It's a sunny day and you will soon dry out."

Hidden under a tall bank and sitting on the trunk of a tree, they listened to the sound of battle and waited for it to end. Periodically Sam broke the foliage cover with a delicate hand and looked up-river. The great Williamite army was now advancing down the slopes of Tullyallen Hill and moving across the river with some ease

But they were not totally remote from the battle. The water which flowed beneath them was red and frequently a dead soldier would float past, blood flowing from a wound. Jimmy looked sadly at the wet corpses carried carelessly by, insignificant under the light of the warm sun.

* * * * *

John Desmond had slept fitfully after his journey from Dublin. Now he was awake. A cannon ball ploughed into the earth beside him, destroying a camp and tearing the arm from a soldier. He watched as the man rushed passed him, blood pouring from his shoulder. For a moment he thought that he might vomit onto the grass. It was his first taste of battle. His horse shied and tried to break its reins. He was disturbed by the confusion.

By now the whole camp was stirring. John Desmond had a chance to look across the river at Tullyallen Hill. Great guns with long snouts thundered out against the Jacobite ranks. Masses of men were moving into position. He watched them move down the hill, cross the river under scorching fire, and secure the village of Oldbridge.

He watched men die. In the distance they were as small as puppets but the screams, the terror, the sight of a bayonet tearing a man's stomach apart frightened him. Everywhere soldiers were strapping on their swords and pistols and preparing to take part in the battle. The left wing of the army had been engaged but now the centre would be called into action as the battle-front widened. Down the far hill soldiers marched on into the river. They were torn by gunfire from the entrenchments and men fell backwards into the river. But the others retained their order and pushed on and swarmed onto the banks.

"Our soldiers will not stand up to them. William's men are hardened in war. They have been under fire before," an officer said as he studied them with his telescope.

The whole field seemed to be moving into battle. Everywhere along the river the regiments and battalions of William were pushing forward in a general movement. Nothing could stop their advance.

Behind Donore Hill a thousand cavalry mustered, waiting for orders to move forward and push William's army back across the river. They moved forwards in great ordered waves. They gathered speed on the hill slope and thundered towards the dense square formation of William's Dutch Guards, massed and thick and ready. They had placed their bayonets on their muskets and formed a pointed wall of steel. As the cavalry descended upon them they discharged their muskets in ordered volleys. Having thrown the horses into confusion and broken the lines of charge they stood firm. The necks and chests of horses were torn by the bayonets and as soldiers fell to the ground they were trampled upon. Still the Dutch Guards held firm.

The cavalry soldiers were ordered to retreat and reform. While they did so the Dutch Guards rammed powder into the muzzles of their guns, loaded them with ball in clockwork fashion and were ready for the second charge which had less energy and force. They picked off the the cavalry as they came down the hill and used the bayonets with the force and effectiveness of disciplined troops. From the northern hill William watched intently as his forces took the brunt of what James could send against him. He now knew that he would win the battle.

John Desmond recognised his brothers as they rode into battle. He cried to them but his voice was drowned by the thunder of hooves and the voices of men. So great was the confusion amongst the cavalry that John Desmond could not see his brothers in the retreat. He screamed out their names. Then he caught sight of his eldest brother. He was wounded. He fell from his horse and the horses' hooves bore down upon him. John Desmond screamed again. Then he began to cry as he saw his brother's broken body on the trampled earth.

His taste for battle ended at that moment. With it ended his wish to dress as a soldier, mount a horse and ride forward to the sound of fife and drum. He wished he were at home at their castle with his mother and his father. And then he looked anxiously for his father. He had once such confidence in him that he believed no ball or bayonet could harm him. Now it was a different matter. On this great field of battle his father was as vulnerable as the common soldier and stood as little chance of surviving.

His thoughts full of fear and worry were shattered by an explosion nearby. A keg of powder had blown up and torn several men apart. Mangled bodies ripped asunder lay close at hand. He retched onto the ground.

"Well soldier lad, what regiment are you with? You dally and vomit while the field is lost," a rough captain said to him. "Mount your horse and follow me. Don't you see that William's army is moving across the river.

Mount and move forward for a charge."

He took John Desmond by the nape of his neck and flung him towards his horse. He watched him mount.

"Here. Take this sword. You will learn how to use it in battle. Now move forward to the left," he said, handing him a sword which he had taken from the shredded body of a man. The blade and handle were wet with blood. John Desmond was confused. He followed the captain forward through the mass and the mess of battle. It was evident that James's troops could not contain the firm and determined power of William's forces. John Desmond watched as raw recruits to James's army threw down their arms and rushed up Donore Hill away from the scene of battle, their eyes bulging with terror.

John Desmond, with a heavy blood-wet sword in his hand, was drawn into the line of battle. It was almost twelve o'clock. The sun burned down upon them from a hot and cloudless sky. Already men's bodies and tongues were dry and rough. As John Desmond looked across the river he could see the final flank of William's army moving into position. The battle was now stretched across a mile front.

John Desmond did not know who gave the order to charge. But suddenly the word was called out and he was carried forward by the others. His little horse whinnied with excitement. He held the sword weakly in his hand. Men were roaring with blood-lust beside him. Their faces were charged with madness. The great force carried him forward. And then as men poured out of the Boyne there was the clash and tangle of steel. Horses shied in confusion and came down with shod hooves on enemy and ally. He looked for an enemy as his horse turned and twisted. There was a gap in the confusion. He kneed his horse through it. He was on the Boyne bank. He looked about him. He watched a soldier take aim with a pistol. And then there was darkness.

The body of John Desmond fell into the river. It was at a deep spot, well-banked. It was drawn downstream.

"Look," said Jimmy Wright. "It's a boy," as he pointed to the body moving past them.

"Let him be. He is one of the enemy. Don't draw attention to us. This battle has gone on too long a time. I hope our luck don't run out, so don't be testing it with pity."

But Jimmy Wright had moved forward through the sally tree and caught the body as it passed beneath him. Sam Gault then drew it into their hiding place.

"A young foolish lad like yourself," he said looking at the boy. "And badly wounded."

A gash ran across his temple. It poured blood.

"He is lucky. A hair's breadth nearer and he would not have lived to tell the tale. I'd better bind the wound," Sam Gault said practically. He was an expert at binding wounds. He took part of John Desmond's fine shirt and tore it into strips. Then he bound it about the head and staunched the flow of blood.

"He's not one of ours," Sam Gault said when he had finished the work. "We should have let him float on down the river. Let his own take care of him. And he belongs to a rich family. Feel the quality of the cloth. Silk and satin." He ran his fingers over the cloth.

"But we must show pity, Sam."

"I know. I know. But who has ever shown pity to me since this battle began except my friend King William. I wonder where he is now. He's the best of men is King William."

"Well I'm sure he is thinking about you," Jimmy Wright said sarcastically.

"He probably is. He probably is," Sam Gault replied seriously.

8

Victory and Defeat

ing William was close at hand but he had little thought for Sam Gault. More weighty considerations filled his mind. The battle was now running in his favour. He had stretched his father-in-law's forces to their limit. Now he would lead his cavalry across the river. William was too weak to carry his sword. In his hand he had a walking stick. And his asthma had choked his chest. He drew shallow breaths as his horse entered the water. Half way across he had to dismount in mid stream and wade ashore. It tested his strength. But once mounted on the far side he felt new energy. He now knew that he had James's troops caught, like fish, in a spread net. He would draw the ends together.

But as he looked towards the hill, he saw the weary Jacobite cavalry regroup. His quick eye placed their number at a little above a thousand. They had endured the rigours of battle for two hours under a hot sun. Both they and their horses were weary of the charges and savage encounters. William ordered his own fresh cavalry troops forward. Again and again the Jacobite cavalry charged. Finally, too weary to attempt another charge, they retired to the summit of Donore Hill.

It was obvious to James that he had been deceived by William's ploy. He had moved the greater part of his army four miles away, to the point from which he expected the main attack. All morning they had remained inactive, facing a Williamite force across an impossible boggy marsh. James now knew that the battle was over. They must escape through the narrow funnel left by William's army.

From all over the field weary Jacobite soldiers began to move towards Duleek, casting aside weapons as they went. They looked bedraggled and horror filled their faces. Periodically, they looked backwards to see if William's army was bearing down upon them. Some fled from the main lines and made for the refuge of the woods and the hills.

The sun was high and beat down upon the confused and straggling army. They desired water and rest.

All day the retreat lasted. William deliberately let the defeated enemy escape. He had no wish to take his father-in-law prisoner. He believed that James would now flee back to France and forget his claim to the throne. England would be secure for a Protestant succession. Ulster would be certain in its allegiance. The old Catholic cause was now in shreds.

And finally, after a long day, the sun began to set over the living, the wounded and the dead. The retreat was almost final. William made his way to Duleek where he was shown James's baggage, which included a silver dinner service. He pushed further towards Naul but decided to return to Duleek. A coach was waiting for William. He would sleep at Duleek. He said goodnight to his officers and closed the door on the long day's events. All over the battlefield William's soldiers, weary after the events of the day, were wrapping themselves in their cloaks and preparing to sleep. Further south the retreat continued.

Sam Gault's muscles ached. He had sat on the hard trunk for six hours while the battle raged above him. He was wet and now he was becoming cold and querulous. He watched the shadows of the sally tree lengthen on the water. It was obvious to him that the battle was now over. No corpses passed down before his eyes and the water had cleared itself of blood. Voices came and went along the bank above them and he listened to every snatch of conversation to pick up news of the battle. It was evident by six o'clock that William had won and that James had taken flight.

Jimmy Wright was also shivering with cold and fear gripped his heart. He looked at his drum, secure in the branches, and vowed that he would never crackle a battle beat on it again.

It was towards evening that John Desmond became a little lucid.

To the question "Who are you?" he answered his name.

"I am John Desmond," he said, but then he went on to speak of five brothers and a father who had taken part in the battle on James's side. It did not make sense to Sam Gault.

"His mind is wandering. What call would he have to join the battle. All we can do is lift him on to the bank and hope somebody will claim him."

"But he may die, Sam."

"We all may die if everything is considered. We have done more than we should. More than we should."

They watched the light thin. The sun was calm and large and red on the horizon. They watched the rim pass down beyond the sky. It was soon dark.

"Time for me to move through the battlefield and find out what has happened," Sam Gault told Jimmy Wright. "I'll give a low whistle when I return."

He dragged himself up the bank, gasping and muttering as he clawed into the earth. He peered into the darkness before he finally committed himself to the firm ground. He gazed about him. He was well acquainted with the night and found it easy to discern shapes. Everywhere he heard were the groans of the wounded as they cried out for water and help.

He had to stop his ears to the groans. It was ever thus after battles. His eyes were keen. He had often moved though battlefields at night when they had been deserted by the living. Already, the scavengers had moved out of the seclusion of the woods and were moving furtively among the corpses. They were dark featureless figures from a shadowy world. But Sam Gault was in search of hard information. His progress was slow through the mass of dead men and horses and the hard shapes of abandoned cannon.

Finally he saw a small camp-fire and some soldiers gathered about it. They had drawn cloaks about their backs, for the summer night brought a chill. Their backs were hooped and they talked of the the events of the day, each trying to recall some vivid image to build up a picture of what had occurred. But already they had heard of the fortunes of the Desmond family. Five sons and a father had been killed that day. They considered how these things happen and how the dice of chance is sometimes thrown with favour and many times with disfavour.

"Who goes there?" one called sharply, aiming a pistol at the figure of Sam Gault.

"Friend of King William and fifer to the Dutch Blue Guard," Sam Gault cried in a croaking voice, fearing that now he had survived the battle he would be killed by a loose pistol shot.

"Then advance to be recognised."

Sam Gault advanced into the light.

"Sit down," the soldiers said roughly, "and

tell us what you witnessed of the battle."

Sam Gault had a strong imagination. During the next half-hour he described charges which had never taken place and the dangers he had encountered. In return he discovered much of what had happened during the day. It was only towards the end that he heard the story of the Desmond family.

"All killed?" he asked.

"All killed," they replied. Even the hardened soldiers were touched by such a terrible catastrophe.

"And where did the Desmonds live?" he asked.

"Somewhere close to Dublin, so the story goes. They come from a castle."

"I see, I see," Sam Gault muttered.

As he returned across the dark battlefield he noticed that the sounds of the dying had decreased. It was deep night. The stars were lustrous over the battlefield, definite in their eternal positions. Sam Gault, standing amongst the dead and observing the heavens, knew that it was a good thing to be alive.

Already a plan was forming in his head. He discovered a large cannon and found a long rope attached to the base. This he cut with his knife.

He whistled as he reached the bank of the river. He waited for a moment and there was an answering whistle. He lay on the bank of the river and called down to Jimmy Wright.

"We have the place to ourselves. There is no need to fear. James has fled and so has his army. I'll let down a rope and you can tie it to the Desmond boy. Then we will hoist him onto the ground."

It took them some time to raise the young boy on to the bank of the Boyne. He lay unconscious between them.

"We are bringing the lad to Dublin, Jimmy Wright," Sam Gault said stolidly.

"Dublin? But I thought that you would have no truck with Dublin," Jimmy Wright commented in a surprised voice.

"I've changed my mind," he answered stiffly.

"But you said nothing would change your mind. You told me that the world ends at the edge of the Boyne. We don't belong in Dublin."

Clearly Jimmy Wright was irritating Sam Gault.

"That was so before I heard of this lad's family." And with that he told him what he had learned.

"So what are your plans?" Jimmy Wright asked.

"We will wait until the first dawn."

While they waited the scavengers moved across the battlefield, robbing the corpses. They were like figures of death in a chapbook print. As the light whitened on the horizon they melted from the battlefield.

Jimmy Wright looked at the carnage about him. Everywhere dead bodies littered the ground in grotesque positions. The limbs were growing stiff, the flesh pale. Blood was hardening in wounds. Here and there dogs were moving through the corpses, licking blood-puddles. The small areas where the battle had been most intense were marked by tangled bodies and horses. But Sam Gault noted that all life had not been destroyed on the battlefield. A small pup whined close by. There was no reason why it should have been on the field of battle. He took it up between thumb and finger and tickled its wet nose. It licked his finger.

"I'll raise this pup to a dog," he told Jimmy and he placed him inside his leather jerkin. "And now I must find us a horse and a cart."

He moved quickly through the litter of corpses. He was away for an hour. When he returned, he told Jimmy Wright that he had secured a horse and cart.

"Nothing great, but enough to get us to Dublin. Take my fife and bring your drum. I'll carry the lad to the cart. He lifted the half-conscious boy on his back and made his way slowly across the dense battlefield. Finally they reached the end of the dead bodies and there tied to a tree was an old horse with yellow teeth, and a cart nearby. They placed John Desmond on some hay, made sure he was comfortable, and moved forward down the road to Duleek. It was very early and the soldiers had not yet moved.

As Sam Gault looked at the brightening sky and the silver dew on the grass and listened to bird-song, his heart lightened. He took out his flute, blew into it and rid it of Boyne dust, then he began to play the Lillibulero. Jimmy Wright hooked his drum to his leather belt and joined in. The music lifted their hearts.

At Duleek the saw a great coach at the side of the road surrounded by officers who stood stiffly to attention. Within, William of Orange was awakened to the sound of the fife and drum music.

He yawned and opened the window of the carriage. Sam Gault was passing by.

"Good morning, Sam Gault," he called.

"Good morning, King William," Sam Gault called back.

"You survived then?"

"Yes, Your Majesty, both hanging and battle fire."

"Then you are a lucky man, Sam Gault. And where go you now?"

"Down the road to Dublin."

"Then good morning to you, Captain Sam Gault, for you deserve to be called Captain."

"Thank you Your Majesty. A good morning and a good day to you."

"We shall not meet again, Captain Sam Gault."

"No, Your Majesty. Goodbye Your Majesty."

"And goodbye to you, Captain Sam Gault."

Captain Sam Gault fifed on down the road to Dublin. King William watched the small retreating figure of great significance and of no significance at all. Great captains and counts hâd been killed on the battlefield. The fifer had survived.

* * * * *

"All dead?" she asked blankly.

"Yes, Lady Desmond," the messenger told

her.

"And John?"

"We have no news of him. Perhaps he never reached the battlefield."

The enormity of the news was too great for her charged heart. Her whole family had been wiped out in a battle of one day. Her head was heavy with grief and she could not weep. She stared blankly through the window at the garden where she had walked with her husband only a short time previously.

Her mind worked mechanically. She turned from the window and said to the messenger.

"I shall send my servants with you to the field of battle. See that the bodies are decently coffined and carry them home to Desmond Castle. They will be interred in the family crypt."

Two days later they were brought home. Six carts carried them up the great avenue. Very few attended the burial. Dublin was in confusion and men were changing their allegiance.

When the coffins had been sealed in the great vault, Lady Desmond retired to her room. She refused to eat or to converse with anybody. She sat in her armchair and stared down the avenue. She did not notice evening passing into night and the dawn brought her no joy.

* * * * *

For Sam Gault the road to Dublin was not an easy one. The horse was old and tired and moved only slowly. Then the wound on John Desmond's head opened and the bandage carried a long fresh stain. The young boy became delirious. They led the cart from the road and rested in a wood. It took a whole day to staunch the blood. When night descended Sam Gault went in search of food. Later he returned with a pitcher of milk and a loaf of bread, stolen from some unsuspecting farmer. He forced the half-conscious boy to drink the milk. Then he sat down and, having given Jimmy Wright part of the bread, munched the larger part reflectively. Their progress towards Dublin was slow.

And next morning when they reached the road, they discovered that part of William's army was moving down in front of them.

"I hope that we are not caught in another battle," Sam Gault muttered angrily. "We have done our part."

The summer's day was hot. The land was dry and hard and the pounding of horses' hooves set up a thick corridor of dust along the road. It irritated the eyes and made them weep and filled the nostrils and the mouth with its fine grit. Sam Gault drew the horse and cart into the long train of wagons and followed them.

In the meantime John Desmond lay still and weak on the hay. Jimmy Wright sat beside him with a wet rag. With this he sponged the burning forehead to keep it cool. He felt that the young boy was dying. His skin was chalk-white and he seemed to have fallen into a deep sleep. Jimmy Wright felt that they must hurry. They had lost a day on the road and Dublin seemed nowhere in sight.

That night when the army pitched its camp in Swords, Sam Gault remained with them. They had encountered no enemy and most felt that the campaign was over.

That night Sam Gault left the camp and stole into the darkness. He felt afraid in the strange landscape where the accents were different and where most of the population spoke Irish. He wandered about in the darkness until he came to a road. He walked along it for some time He noticed the dim outline of a village in a dip of ground and he went down the slope in search of information.

He knocked on one of the small doors. No one moved within. Then he moved to another.

Then some one sprang upon him and held a dagger to his throat.

"A prowling Williamite," the voice said in English "What brings you here?"

"I cannot speak with a dagger at my gullet," Sam Gault replied.

The pressure of the knife-blade was eased and Sam Gault drew his breath.

"I'm looking for directions to Castle Desmond or some such place," he said.

"Why?"

"Because I have brought a young Desmond lad from the Boyne and he needs attention. The young lad has lost a great amount of blood."

"All the Desmond men are dead. They were buried to-day. You lie," the voice said.

"One remains, I tell you. A young lad, John. I could have let him drown in the river. I had no call to come trooping here to Dublin. I have all to lose."

"Then come with me," the voice said and with a dagger pushed at his back Sam Gault moved forward. A door was opened and he was pushed in. A small light flickered and showed the faces of several Jacobite captains.

Some of them were wounded but most were sitting about a rough table.

"Who have we got here?" one of the captains asked.

"A prowler whose throat I should have cut. But he is witness to a strange tale," the officer said.

"What is your name?" the commanding officer demanded.

"Sam Gault."

"Your rank?"

"No rank."

"Occupation?"

"Fifer and gravedigger."

"And what brings you to Dublin?"

"A foolish heart," and with that he told the whole story of what had happened, even his conversation with William of Orange.

"And what was William doing at that early hour of the morning?"

"Putting on his trousers and preparing to eat a better breakfast than Sam Gault," Sam said in anger. One of the officers made to strike him. But the commanding officer stayed his hand.

"You are a man of courage, Sam Gault," he said.

"I'm weary and I wish I were a hundred

miles from the tail-end of this battle," he replied.

"Then tell us of William's forces," one of them asked.

"What can I tell you? They were at the Boyne two days ago and now they are here. Surely you have seen for yourselves. I tell you a young lad dies in a cart and you ask me questions I cannot answer."

"A young lad you said. A John Desmond?"

"That is correct."

They spoke amongst themselves in Irish. Then they turned to him.

"We will send a young soldier with you dressed as a peasant. He will direct you to Desmond Castle. If he does not return, then there will be a price upon your head, Sam Gault."

Accompanied by the young man Sam Gault staggered up the incline. Clearly there was no end to his adventures. He was a long way from Carrickfergus and his life was surrounded by confusion.

The morning was a grey cuticle of light when Sam Gault returned to the camp with the young soldier. Men were sleeping on the ground with great cloaks wrapped about them.

"He's confused of mind," Jimmy Wright said when they arrived back

"Then we must make haste before he dies upon us," Sam Gault ordered. "Tackle the horse and prepare to move."

Very soon they were ready. They moved through the tents and the sleeping bodies and made their way on to the road.

The young soldier knew his way. Half way down the road they swung to the left. They moved for a mile along a narrow lane covered with trees in deep summer leaf. It was the first time they had been under calm cover since they left Carrickfergus. The woods on either side were filled with scents and they felt at this point that the Battle of the Boyne had ended for them. Their minds became settled and now there was an urgency to get the boy home.

The small road gave way to a wider one. It was close to the sea and to the left was the large brooding shape of Howth. They moved down along the road until they came to a walled estate.

"I leave you here," the young soldier said. "James may have fled but I have to continue the fight under Patrick Sarsfield. We may be beaten at the Boyne but our victories will come west of the Shannon." With that he jumped from the cart, waved goodbye and walked away from them.

Sam Gault and Jimmy Wright then passed in awe through the great ornamental gates and the granite pillars bearing a coat of arms. Their awe increased as they moved up the avenue and the castle came into sight. The old horse continued, drawing the cart forward with difficulty. They drew up the cart on the gravel before the great doors. They waited.

Lady Desmond watched the dawn break over Dublin Bay. It was an empty dawn and brought her no delight. She wished that the night would continue so that she could stare into the darkness for an infinity. There was nothing left to live for. All her family had been destroyed in the terrible turmoil.

And then towards morning she saw a strange sight. An old horse and cart with a small, wizened driver in a leather jerkin and a boy with a drum made their way up the avenue. She stared at their slow progress. They stopped on the gravel. In the back of the cart on a bed of hay lay her son, John. She was suddenly filled with energy. She rushed from the room, called to the servants and hurried down the stairs.

Sam Gault and Jimmy Wright were surprised when the doors were thrown open and the servants, both men and women, rushed out. They thought for a moment that they might be set upon and driven from the grounds.

"It is Master John. It is Master John," they kept repeating. "He is alive."

Reverently they lifted him from the pallet of hay and carried him indoors. Wisps still clung to his clothes. Only a tall lady remained outside. Her eyes were blue and surrounded by the dark shadows of sorrow. Sam Gault knew that this was Lady Desmond who had lost a husband and so many sons.

"You carried my son all the way from the field of battle?" she asked directly.

"Yes, My Lady," Sam Gault said.

"And how did you know he was my son and how did you discover Desmond Castle?" she asked.

"It is a long story," Sam Gault replied.

"Then you must tell me all about it. Come inside and I will have the servants attend to you."

A servant took the old horse and cart with some disdain and brought it to the yard. Sam Gault and Jimmy Wright mounted the steps of the great house and entered the great hall. They had never been in so large and wonderful a place before and they were mute with surprise. A servant brought them to the kitchen with its arched roof and set them to eat. Their food had been rough and scarce for so long a time that they nibbled at the bread until their appetites returned. But when the taste of good food was on their mouths they ate ravenously and with relish.

"Best meal I ever had, Jimmy," Sam said when he had cleared his plate. "I have only been in Dublin a day and I fare better than in Carrickfergus."

"Don't forget your manners. Mrs. McGuzzle always said that you could judge a man by his manners. You surely do not wish to be thrown out on your neck and head."

"Indeed no."

"You have a most peculiar accent!" one of the servants laughed.

"King William and King James found nothing wrong with it," Sam Gault retorted.

"You knew both kings?" she asked in awe.

"Both friends of mine." And with that Sam began to spin a fine tissue of lies into a lively tale. Jimmy Wright felt quite embarrassed on account of his friend.

Meanwhile, in the wide bedroom on the second storey Lady Desmond removed the bandage from her son's head and looked at the wound above the ear. It was blue and bloodless. She cleaned away the dirt and bound it again. With the help of the servants she encouraged her son to drink some honey. She spoke quiet words of encouragement to him while she poured the honey through his lips. He recognised her voice, opened his eyes for a moment and then fell back into his coma. Then they placed his head on a silken pillow and he began to sleep deeply.

Lady Desmond was anxious, but now she knew that he would recover.

When she came down the wide stairs she asked one of the servants to bring Sam Gault and Jimmy Wright to the library. Sam Gault in the presence of the lady realised that he could neither exaggerate or tell lies. So he told the story of what happened, beginning at the very first moment when they sighted William of Orange to the moment when they arrived in front of the great house.

"And what do you intend to do now?" she asked.

"Wait for the smoke of the battle to blow away and then return to Carrickfergus."

"Well, I invite you both to stay as long as you wish," she said. "Rooms will be prepared for you and you will receive new clothes."

"Thank you very much, Lady Desmond," Jimmy Wright said, remembering Mrs. McGuzzle's words.

*   *   *   *   *

They never left the house or the estate. Jimmy Wright became companion to John Desmond. He was given a pony and he was taught how to ride. He assumed polite ways and grew to be a young gentleman.

Sam Gault was given a small house on the estate and this was a source of great pride to him. Periodically, when the urge came upon him, he took his fife and played through the streets of Dublin. Sometimes he disappeared for whole months and made his way to Waterford or Galway. But he always returned to the estate. He maintained that he was a Belfast man and a Dublin man and a Catholic and a Protestant, which was a safe position to hold but very confusing and he would not argue on the matter.

He cherished one prized possession. It was a pewter mug. Upon it were inscribed the following words:

King William of Orange and Sam Gault from Carrickfergus supped from this goblet.

Sam Gault lived a long life. He died peacefully in his sleep. Jimmy Wright had the following words carved upon his tombstone:

Captain Samuel Gault, Fifer to the King.

Children's
POOLBEG

The Viking Princess

by

Michael Mullen

"Would make a great film"

Evening Herald

£2.99